Sentimental Journey

Cheryl Barnett
Alger Olson

SterlingHouse

Pittsburgh, PA

ISBN 1-56315-195-2

Paperback Fiction
© Copyright 1999 Cheryl Kay Barnett-Alger Olson
All rights reserved
First Printing—1999
Library of Congress #98-85325

Request for information should be addressed to:

SterlingHouse Publisher, Inc.
The Sterling Building
440 Friday Road
Department T-101
Pittsburgh, PA 15209

Cover design & typesetting: Drawing Board Studios

Printed in Canada

Linda F. Logman who was a
'driving' force behind this book .

and to

Colonel Richard S. Hagen who
introduced us to the mysteries
of England.

Chapter 1

The Cottage

The whitewashed cottage with its green, lichen encrusted slate roof, nestled cosily along the smooth flowing Avon River was all that the travel agent said it would be except for... but that's getting ahead of our story.

The agent, affectionately known as Cheerio among Centre College staff was adamant. "Cottages, especially those in England, make enchanting retreats," she had said with an air of familiarity. "The one you are looking at is a new listing, but from the description—two bedrooms, bath in each one, fully equipped kitchen, laundry facilities and two fireplaces, one in a paneled study and the other in the living room— should be perfect for you and Clay."

"The fax doesn't give an age, but I bet the cottage is over 300 years old and if you decide to take it, a Mrs. Simmons who lives in Morning Meadow writes that she will meet you on the 15th to help you get your hair dryers and shavers to work, as well as offering a bit of instruction on the operation of her country's baffling flush toilets.

And so it was that Morgan and Clay Ashton decided that the first two weeks of Morgan's semester-long sabbatical would be spent in historic Stratford-Upon-Avon, where John Barnett, a distant relative of Morgan's had lived, she had heard, prior to emigrating to the Virginia Colony around 1720.

Traffic on the M40 heading north out of London had been heavy due to miles of road construction, and it was late afternoon when Clay, after several stops for directions, turned onto the gravel driveway that fronted the cottage upon the Avon.

"Do you like it?" Clay asked, somewhat breathlessly while dropping the first of a half dozen bulging suitcases on the flagstone floor with a resounding thud.

"Like it? I love it." Morgan had already disappeared into a room just off the hall. "Hurry, Clay, come see this wonderfully inviting room. It must be the study—and look, someone has kindled a fire and there's a bottle of pink champagne on the desk. Mrs. Simmons must be about. Come look out this window; the Avon flows right past our back door, and there are two white swans circling in the water."

Clay put his arms around his wife's waist. "Are you happy darling?"

"Yes, yes, yes. I've waited ten long years for this sabbatical and to find our dream cottage in the process ... yes I'm very happy."

After unpacking their suitcases, Clay, looking tired, combined a kiss with a "goodnight sweetheart," and disappeared under a thick patchwork quilt that rested atop their sagging four poster bed. Morgan smiled as she watched her husband turn over and fall fast asleep.

Parting the lace curtains and swinging open the bedroom's only window, she watched the waters of the Avon, that shimmered under the light of a pale moon, glide quietly by. "Dreams do come true," she said softly as she closed and locked it again. Except for the mellow glow of a shaded night light, the room was dark and still. Standing barefoot on the flagstone floor, she was about to pull back the covers when from within the cottage came the sound of the front door opening, followed by the soft, lilting sound of a woman laughing. For a long moment she stood transfixed, her body taut, her heart pounding. Clay had not moved and the house was again still.

They had inspected every nook and cranny, and it was absurd to think that someone could have escaped their notice and be hiding in the house. Shivering, she climbed into bed and for a long time lay listening. Except for an occasional crack or thump, the house remained silent. Snug under the covers, she wondered if the sounds she had heard were real or the creation of an overactive imagination. Eventually, her fear subsided and she breathed a tired sigh and drifted off to sleep.

The next morning after a leisurely breakfast, Clay, upon giving Morgan a kiss on the tip of her nose, left for Stratford in search of an electrical converter that would accomodate their shavers and hair dryer.

Throughout breakfast, Morgan had been noticeably quiet, prompting Clay to ask somewhat anxiously if something was bothering her. "You don't mind staying alone for a little while?" he asked, touching her shoulder.

"No, you go. I'm fine, it just takes me awhile to get used to strange houses," she replied, giving Clay a wan smile. The sounds she had heard last night had frightened her badly and she wondered if she should accompany Clay. "No," she told herself. She would stay and write several letters and fill several vases she had found with flowers that grew in glorious profusion around the cottage. A bit of color, she thought, would help alleviate the disquieting feeling that had overtaken her.

Clay, his mission accomplished, appeared so quietly that Morgan, who sat at the huge mahogany desk with her back to the study window, hadn't heard him come in. "I'm sorry if I startled you, honey," Clay said apologetically. "I thought you were dozing and I didn't want to disturb you."

"Your apology is not sufficient. Come give me a hug," Morgan said, giving Clay a keen look and holding our her arms that trembled ever so slightly.

The slanting afternoon sun felt good on her back and helped to dispell the chill that had invaded the room. "Clay," Morgan asked after a long moment of silence, "do you think it was Mrs. Simmons who was here yesterday and started the fire? If she did, I wonder what happened to her? If she had to leave, I would think she would have left a note or something."

Morgan's questions, uttered just above a whisper, seemed almost detached as she sat cradling her chin in her hands, eyes riveted on a blue, leather-bound book she had found on the desk.

The tone of her questions was all too familiar to Clay, who over the past five years, had come to realize that his wife's questions were not only eminently purposeful, but often contained unspoken clues to her thinking.

Placing another log on the fire, he watched a stream of glowing embers disappear up the chimney. For a moment, his thoughts returned to a misty morning in early September, 1989, when he and Morgan had strolled along a deserted stretch of beach at Murrells Inlet, South Carolina. The wind had been up, and with the tide rising the ocean had the look of old pewter. It had been one of their rare driving vacations. They had first spent a week visiting Morgan's brother at Charleston, and then had driven up to Myrtle Beach to enjoy of few days of golf before she would go back to the inevitable intellectual skirmishing and ancient predjudices that had marked her tenure as Professor of Speculative Religions at Centre College.

Clay too was not terribly anxious to get back to the nagging familiar world of media advertising. In his ten years in the business-the last five as Director Accounts Management for Poole & Davis, a large and respected firm in St. Paul, he had come to accept the intrigues, the prickly prides, the exaggerated perceptions, and the corporate knifings as a rite of passage. Financial success had somewhat tempered his frustrations and disillusionments. Over the intervening years, due to his skill for incisive, illuminating and revelational presentations to richly endowed corporate partisans, he had become indespensible to the firm.

As they had walked along the beach that morning, watching the gulls swoop over the rollers, he remembered how suddenly Morgan had gripped his arm a little tighter. It wasn't until they had returned to their hotel and were dressing for dinner that Morgan asked his impression of the tall man wearing a long grey coat and a slouch hat that they had passed along the beach. Clay had seen no one. "But you must have seen him," Morgan protested. "He passed not five feet from us." Later, upon questioning the hotel manager, they were told that a man fitting Morgan's description and known by the locals as the Grey Man was often seen on that stretch of the beach just before a hurricane. It was thought that he brought good fortune to anyone who saw him. On September 21, Hurricane Hugo, packing winds of 135 miles per hour, had slammed into the coast of South Carolina, creating a night of death and terror.

It wasn't the first time that Morgan had either felt or seen what might be described as a ghostly presence that Clay had not. There had been at least a dozen other instances of sightings that had eluded Clay's senses altogether. His mother had once remarked that when she was young she thought she had seen her father sitting in his favorite rocking chair reading a newspaper long after he had died, but because his dad had taken such a cold and dispassionate view of ghosts, the subject was never brought up again. While he took Morgan's strange and often startling experiences seriously, he could not totally accept what he could not explain. Morgan's questions regarding the whereabouts of Mrs. Simmons again raised in his mind the unattractive and all too familiar suspicion that she had again tuned into something that might prove to be disquieting.

"I agree that Mrs. Simmons' absence is a bit puzzling," Clay said, turning away from the fire, "but to hint that there is something peculiar about her truancy stretches it a bit, don't you think?"

"Possibly," Morgan replied without looking up, "but I do feel that this cottage, and especially this room, holds many secrets. Come look at this book, for instance. It was sitting here on the desk. There's no title or any clue to its publisher, but the entire book is written in the most beautiful handwriting I have ever seen."

Clay, who had been examining what appeared to be a series of beautifully bound Dickens' first editions in a cherry book case opposite the fireplace, quietly closed the case's glass doors and sat down in a wing-backed chair across the desk from his wife.

"Listen to this." Morgan's voice seemed to quiver with excitement as the two exchanged glances. "On October 26, 1939, a Mr. Owen Bates, vicar of St. James, a rural church in Warwickshire, left home by car with the express purpose of visiting his elderly sister in Swindon. His last known whereabouts occurred when he stopped in Oxford to have lunch with a fellow graduate of Queen's College. Oxford isn't that interesting," Morgan said, glancing up and giving Clay a quizzical look. "To the mortification of his sister, his colleagues, and parishioners," she continued, "the highly esteemed Mr. Bates has not been seen again. The constabulary conducted a thorough search of the roads between Oxford and Swindon as well as adjacent communities. Foul play was suspected, but never proved. Mr. Bates and his car have simply vanished. Here's another entry. A Miss Hillary Bowden, a tutor of Experimental Physics, left her apartment in Oxford on May 2, 1963, telling friends she would be spending the weekend with relatives and attending a lecture on wildwood flowers at the Tropical Bird Gardens in Bath. When she failed to appear at her regularly scheduled tutoring sessions on Monday, the college's proctors were asked to investigate. Questions about Miss Bowden's whereabouts would go unanswered. She had not stopped to visit her brother in Bath as she was expected to. Her sister, too, had no idea where she might have gone. According to her colleagues, it was totally out of character for her to miss a tutoring session and if she had been delayed or had car trouble, she surely would have notified the college's administrators. The local constabulary conducted a thorough search of the roads she'd been expected to travel without success. Miss Bowden and her car had mysteriously disappeared."

Even with a cheery fire crackling on the grates, the room had grown noticeably cooler. Her eyes still fixed on the book, Morgan hugged her baggy wool sweater around her a little tighter. "Clay, this entire book is filled with strange and unexplained disappearances and each chapter is complete and composed in a different handwriting. What do you think it means? Clay...where are you?"

The question dissolved in the shrill ring of the telephone.

"It's Cheerio," Clay called from the kitchen. "She wants to know how we like the cottage."

"Tell her we haven't had time to get fully acquainted," Morgan murmured somewhat uneasily.

"Cheerio says that Mrs. Simmons was here early in the afternoon yesterday. She made the fire and left the champagne and says she apologizes for not being here to welcome us. If we need anything or have trouble with appliances, heating and such, we should call Alan Crabtree, who lives three cottages to the right. He's a Yorkshireman and Mrs. Simmons says we'll like him. See, didn't I tell you that the truant Mrs. Simmons really does exist?" Clay said, smiling as he reappeared in the doorway holding two glasses of sherry, sipping one as he talked. The telephone call had somewhat quieted his own uneasiness, but he could tell that Morgan was not totally satisfied. Her lips pursed, she seemed absorbed in thought.

A blood red leaf fluttering by the window drew Morgan's attention away from the book to a painting hanging against the highly polished cherry paneling that framed the fireplace. The painting, done on canvas and without signature, presented an idyllic portrait of an English village. In the center stood a pub whose half timbered and gabled upper story overreached a sturdy foundation of rusty colored brick. A steep, chipped stone roof covered with patches of black lichen secured the occupants from the elements and at each end stood two singular round towers capped by cone shaped witches hats. To the left of the pub, an ancient wall, its stones entwined in ivy, followed a meandering path to a steepled church peeping out among a grove of trees. Two inviting, honey-colored thatched cottages with red and pink rambling roses growing over the doorways and windows stood alongside a tree-shaded, mirror-like stream to the right. The pub, whose diamond-shaped windows glowed with a warm light looked out at a man and woman whose faces, in contrast to the rest of the aging portrait seemed freshly painted. Above the arched door a swinging sign board carried the name, *Song O' The Winds.*

" What a lovely picture," Morgan said, walking over to the fireplace to get a closer look.

Clay joining her, nodded his assent. "The artist must have painted it while sitting just about here." His finger pointed to a curious, rounded, blue stone marker that stood like a sentinel at the bottom left edge of the painting.

"I wonder if this village exists somewhere," Morgan's voice was soft and somewhat distant. Her eyes seemed glasslike in the flickering firelight. "I somehow feel connected; it's all so vaguely familiar." Clay handed her a glass of sherry and put his arm around her waist. Morgan half turned and holding the glass in both hands, studied the contents before looking up.

"Clay, did you hear a strange sound in the night?"

Their eyes met. Clay took her glass and was about to set it down on the desk when a loud, booming knock reverberated through the house as if someone had struck a bass drum. Suddenly the front door squeaked open and a deep baritone voice called in from the foyer, "Ellow, is anyone 'ome?"

"Yes, yes come in," Clay called, setting the glasses down. His suprised parting glance hinted that he hadn't heard any disquieting noises in the night.

The man standing in the doorway towered over Clay's 6'1" frame. With his plaid cap firmly clenched in his left hand, he extended his work-hardened right in a firm greeting.

"I'm Alan Crabtree. Come to see if yer gettin' along awright. I've 'ad strict orders from Mrs. Simmons to look after ye. I 'ope everthing is to yer likin'. I see you 'ave a warm fire goin'. Aye, a proper English cottage should always 'ave a cheery fire burnin' to help dispell the dampness."

"We're quite satisfied, thank you," Morgan said somewhat hesitantly. "But then this is only our second day ... Clay, can we offer Mr. Crabtree a cup of tea or something?"

"A spot of tea would do just fine. The weather has taken on a bit of a chill which starts my rheumatism to painin'."

"Come sit by the fire," Morgan said, pulling a chair from across the room. "I understand you're from Yorkshire?"

"Aye. Anyone can tell us Yorkshiremen. We all 'ave round faces; my wife says it's like a plate; our hair is the color of thatch, our noses are long-they say to poke in everybody's business-and our eyebrows are so bushy that a bird can nest in them."

"Well, that's a rather unkind description," Morgan said, studying her guest with increased interest.

"Honey, there's no loose tea in the cupboard, and I'm not sure how many tea bags I should put in the pot." Clay re-entered the room carrying a tray containing a cocoa-brown steaming tea pot and three China cups.

"I think the accepted formula is one bag per cup and one for the pot. Is that true, Mr. Crabtree?" Morgan asked.

"It'll do." The delicately-crafted tea cup nearly disappeared in his massive hand.

"Tell us about the cottage, Mr. Crabtree," Morgan said, pulling her own chair closer to the fire. Clay, standing beside her holding his saucer and cup, gingerly sipped his tea and nodded.

"I'd take it kindly if you would call me Alan; would be more proper like. Hereabouts we like to use a person's first name unless we are in the presence of titled folk, so to speak." There was a slight hint of embarrassment in his voice as he placed his saucered cup on a small, circular table at his elbow.

"About the toilets, now you 'ave to hold down the 'andle for some seconds before the water will go down and Mrs. Simmons wrote that there may be an electrical adapter in the bathroom cupboard that will run your shavers and dryers and such. And...."

"We've solved the toilet mystery and we didn't find an adapter so we purchased one," Clay interrupted as he carried what looked like a terribly uncomfortable, small, leather-bound chair from across the room and sat down next to his wife. "But tell us what you can about this cottage. Who owns it? What is its history? How old is it?" Morgan, her eyes fixed on their guest nodded in agreement.

"Well, I don't know," Alan said, running his hand through his mass of sandy hair. "I was 'ired by Mrs. Simmons to look after things, but for yer questions, I 'ave no good answers. I would say though that the cottage is much older than any other hereabouts."

"Our travel agent said that the cottage was a new listing. Did you know the people who stayed here before we arrived?" Morgan's question came between sips of tea and her hand trembled a bit.

"There has been no one 'ere for the past eight autumns and that's a fact." Alan's voice took on a measured quality. "I was 'ired just a month ago to go in and see that everything was in workin' order, that there were no leaks or damage of any such kind and there weren't." Giving his head a quick downward jerk to emphasize his point, he continued. "Come to think of it, there wasn't much dust around either. The last people who were 'ere were an older couple from London, I think. My misses who visited with the woman said that 'er husband was an actor in Shakespeare plays, but I never got to know them very well and they stayed but a week."

"What is Mrs. Simmons like?" Morgan asked, placing her hand on Clay's arm and giving it a squeeze. "We hear she was here yesterday and lit a fire and left a welcoming bottle of champagne."

Alan looked somewhat startled. "She was 'ere? Mmmmm. Mind I've never met Mrs. Simmons. All our business 'as been done through the post."

"That's odd," Clay said, getting up and walking over to

the fireplace. Picking up a log, he dropped it on the glowing coals.

"She writes me regular, but I've never met the lady. One day about a month ago, a solicitor from town knocks on our door and asks if I would look after this cottage for a month. He did that before the other couple moved in and he said that another couple would be movin' in and that me job would be to see that the appliances worked and that I should look in from time to time to see if they needed anything. And 'ere I am." For a moment the room became deathly quiet. "Well I think I'll be gettin' along," Alan said, picking up his cup for one last sip. "If you need anythin' you'll have to come to our house for we don't 'ave a phone. But I'll look in on you now and again."

"Before you leave, Alan," Morgan said, getting up and lifting Clay's arm at the same time, "I want you to look at this picture hanging above the fireplace. Do you know where this village is and does it seem to you that someone has tampered with the picture by retouching the faces on what seems to be a very old painting?"

Alan approached the fireplace and placed both hands on the mantle. With Morgan and Clay standing beside him, he studied the picture in silence for several minutes. Turning away from the fire, Morgan detected a strange quizzical look in his eyes.

"Mmmm," he began in a half halting way. "I can't be sure, but the man and woman look like the couple who stayed here at the cottage a good while ago."

Chapter 2

The Beginning

Standing in the doorway, Morgan and Clay waved goodbye to Alan, who quickly disappeared in the deepening twilight. The air was crisp and damp, and Morgan shivered as she closed the door and walked quickly across the cold flagstone floor.

"Clay, I'm just shaking." Morgan's voice trembled as she retreated to the cozy warmth of the study. "I can't remember feeling such cold nervousness, it's like... like..."

"It's the dampness," Clay called from the kitchen. "The woman at the car rental agency may have been right when she said England is best known for the two R's-rain and rheumatism. I'm fixing you some hot soup and if you don't mind staying alone for a few minutes, I think I'll drive to the grocers just down the road and pick up something for breakfast. What would you like?"

Snugly engulfed in a thick patchwork quilt with her legs curled under her, Morgan sat facing the fire.

"Don't forget to buy a jar of Cooper's orange marmalade. Cheerio said a proper English breakfast would not be served without it. Besides, it's made in Oxford where we'll be staying for several months."

"I won't forget," Clay said, appearing in the doorway with a tray containing a bowl of steaming vegetable soup, two thick slices of French bread and a cup of hot black tea. "You'll be alright when I'm gone?" Clay's tone betrayed a bit of concern.

"I'll be fine, darling. I'll just sit here by the fire sipping the soup and the tea until you get back."

With Clay gone, the fire again drew Morgan's attention. She watched fingers of blue and yellow flames escape between two badly charred logs. A sudden gust of wind whistled down the the chimney, followed by the sound of rain drumming against the window.

"A perfect night for being alone with your thoughts," Morgan murmured half out loud as she tightened the multi-colored quilt around her shoulders. The fire and the soup had dissolved the clammy chill, and she felt herself being consumed by the drowsy stillness of the room.

Memories, vivid as rainbows after a summer storm filtered across her mind. She remembered how as a child on Sunday mornings in Fincastle, Virginia, her aunt would awaken her in her often sun drenched bedroom.

"Time for church," she would say, picking out a Sunday dress from the closet and laying it on the bed. "God must not be kept waiting."

Her aunt was a pious woman who saw no need for debate or analysis when it came to the scriptures. The path to heaven led straight through her church's front door. The ten commandments in her mind were unmodifiable. "They were commandments, not suggestions," she was fond of saying.

Her uncle John, on the other hand, viewed his wife's tes-timonials of heaven and hell with a sort of cautious amuse-ment. "Emily," he would say, "don't scare the child into heaven. Let her find it for herself."

It wasn't that she disliked attending church on Sundays with her aunt and uncle. She smiled as she recalled how during the sermon many around her would be wistfully gazing off into space. Where were they? Their bodies were in church, but their minds were elsewhere. It was also a source of wonder how people who were models of civility on Sunday mornings could engage in such intemperate habits the rest of the week. Although they were pursuing their promise of paradise along separate paths, she loved both her aunt and uncle deeply. They had raised her when her parents had died within a week of each other due to an automobile accident. She was thirteen at the time and although many years had passed since their deaths, their loving faces had remained fresh in her memory. She reminded herself that she must write to her aunt and uncle, telling them she and Clay had arrived safely and that she intended to see what information she could find on John Barnett. As she stifled a yawn and settled deeper in her chair, her thoughts returned to the cottage. She shivered slightly as she wondered how such pleasant surroundings, which offered every possible comfort could, in addition to the unaccoutable sounds she had heard, produce in her such a strange feeling of unease.

Had she been asleep or did she actually hear someone call the name Duncan Alister from somewhere deep within the house. Startled, Morgan sat upright and noticed that the quilt had fallen off her shoulders. Although the fire still burned bright with an orange and blue flame, the room felt chill as she wrapped the quilt even more tightly around her. The room, except for the usual creaks and groans, seemed quiet enough. A green-shaded reading lamp sitting placidly on a table across from her issued a subdued and inviting light, and the leaping flames from the fire cast a warm, but eerie glow on the surrounding paneling. It was only a dream, she told herself, but her moment of sublime solitude had been broken; her nerves were taut and she wished Clay had not taken so long to get back.

Duncan Alister. Duncan Alister. The name kept echoing in her mind. She hadn't heard Duncan's name mentioned in years. It reminded her of her first interviews with the faculty selection committee at Centre College. Its chairman, Leonard Crawford, Professor and Chair of the Department of Philosophy and Logic, referred to Duncan Alister, the college's founder, as a man deserving of the highest tribute and honor for his vision and faith in a liberal arts education. His credo, according to Leonard, was that given the proper educational atmosphere and training, young and fertile minds, could be motivated to seek universal truths, truths uncluttered by shifting facts and conventional ethics.

The way Leonard had continued to describe the founder in the most reverent and personal way, it seemed to Morgan that he had somehow known Duncan Alister although he must have died long before Leonard was born. She also recalled how unsettled she had felt sitting across the table answering rapid fire questions from five sartorially splendid dressed men and two women who fixed her with a look of calculated superiority. It was Leonard Crawford who would periodically throw back his head and laugh at what he considered to be a question designed to produce a self-destructive response.

"Now, now, professor," he would interrupt, "please reframe your question so that Mrs. Ashton can answer it without fear of self incrimination."

Nearing the close of the interview, she remembered how Leonard had fixed her with a warm and friendly smile and said that she probably would remember little of what was said here, but that he wanted her to give thoughtful attention to her mission, which he said would not only inflame her students' imagination and thirst for knowledge, but to provoke questions and possibly distress as her teachings applied to commonly held beliefs and suppositions. She recalled how the selection committee had sat in stony silence as he told her that brittle intellect should not find a home at Centre.

"Your task, Mrs. Ashton," he had said, "is to send your charges out into the world buttressed not with the feeling of self satisfaction, but with the thought that life tends to be irregular, that doubt is the beginning of wisdom, and that not everything becomes obvious through explanation."

Memories of Leonard were as vivid as the rivulets of water that cascaded down the windows of the study. It was just this sort of evening that she had arrived at Centre to assume her duties as Professor of Religious Studies. Clay had been away on a business trip and in the process of carrying boxes and books from her car to the arched entrance to Old Main, she had gotten thoroughly soaked, leaving puddles of water standing on the warped, darkly stained floor of her office.

She remembered how, out of breath, she had sat down on an uncomfortable, wooden, swivel desk chair and clasped her hands under her chin to survey her tiny second floor office. It had consisted of a recessed ceiling light, a small oak desk, an uncomfortable-looking slatbacked chair and two small oak bookcases with glass-paneled doors. Thick layers of dust covered everything and a graveyard of flies lined the windowsill. Greasy fingerprints dotted two rectangular windows that overlooked the tree lined commons and the bell tower, whose chimes had just struck six.

Muted tones of Beethoven's *Für Elise* had filtered into her office from somewhere down the hall, which helped to relieve the look of melancholy that blanketed her cubicle. It was not what she had expected, but she would not let her Spartan surroundings and the sound of the rain drumming against the windows of her turret-like office diminish her feeling of overwhelming pride that she had achieved one of her most cherished dreams at the age of thirty-eight. She remembered leaning back in her chair and wondering out loud if other professors were billeted in such severe and un-adorned surroundings.

"No they aren't," came the voice of Leonard Crawford, whose 6' 2" frame had filled the doorway. "I hope I didn't startle you. I was reading in my office just down the hall when I heard the thud of a box hitting the floor. I imagined that you had arrived. I sometimes listen to music by candle-light as it seems to enhance the mood of a particular piece. Unfortunately, I have fallen asleep on occasion and Mrs. Michem, the cleaning lady, is afraid that someday I'll set my office on fire. But I know you must be hungry. Would you mind joining me for dinner?"

It was the first of many lunches and dinners they had shared in the ensuing years. She had learned that Leonard was English by birth and had received his doctorate in phi-losophy at Queens College in Oxford. Years of teaching at Centre had, she thought, Americanized his pronunciation, but certain words and phrases still carried the delightful hint of an English accent.

Leonard was not a handsome man. He looked, she thought, like someone one might meet on a hiking trail car-rying a staff and a packsack. His face had a ruddy look, and his dark brown eyes peering out from behind round, wire-rimmed spectacles had a sparkling quality about them. His slightly pink cheeks looked as if they concealed two small plums, and his full lips and wide mouth seemed permanently locked in a knowing smile. Atop his somewhat rounded fea-tures sat a shock of sandy tosseled hair tinged here and there with strands of grey.

Through their subsequent correspondence it was Leonard who had persistently urged her to accept the college's tender of a full professorship in religious studies and it was he who had warned her that her appointment might be met with a gracious chill due, to the fact that certain well established faculty had recommended another person for the position. Later it was Leonard who had suggested that she develop a series of courses on what he called speculative religions which he predicted would unleash a tempest of flippant ridicule, but in the end she would find highly intriguing and revelational.

Morgan's attention was again drawn to the fire, which had in her musings, been reduced to a scattering of glowing coals. The whispers of near transparent smoke drifting lazily up the chimney reminded her of the conversations she and Leonard had had before a similar fire in the college's faculty house uncharitably known as the Old Barn. Invariably, their discussions would devolve to matters of dreams, death, and immortality. Leonard in particular, she thought, seemed preoccupied with these subjects. He had once remarked that while many of the world's religions give assurance of immortality, he wondered if such a promise was more a hope than a conviction.

"One's heaven," she remembered him saying, "lies within the mind rather than the cosmos."

At another of their fireside discussions he had asked her what she thought happens upon death. While the subject of a death and an afterlife had surfaced before, he had not asked her directly for her views.

"I suspect that a part of us survives," she remembered replying. "The soul is the commonly accepted part. There's probably a mansion waiting for us somewhere built to our specified beliefs, values and desires. Sort of our prescription for life."

"Tell me about *your* prescription," Leonard had persisted.

She smiled as she recalled Leonard's talent for unobtrusive questioning.

"Generating an awareness that our minds are capable of inspiring and formulating an infinite number and array of possibilities for our fulfillment and happiness probably best describes my prescription."

She had felt pleasantly satisfied with her answer and remembered looking at her colleague for a sign of acceptance. Instead of the expected response he had raised another and more teasing question.

"Do you think a person must die to obtain eternal life?" He had asked.

She had heard that he had raised the question with some of his students and a number of his colleagues over the years. The question had, as Leonard no doubt anticipated, produced fiery debates among his students. Many of his colleagues, on the other hand, considered the question little more than polished nonsense.

She had not responded directly. She remembered confiding that in her undergraduate days she had become a consummate daydreamer and how, during periods of supreme boredom, she would conjure up and propel herself into wondrous worlds filled with fascinating people and places. No matter how stressful her day had been, her musings had invariably brought about a feeling of peace and contentment. It had occurred to her on several of her sojourns that she could, if she had wished, remain forever in the realms that she had imagined, familiar realms that were increasingly appearing in her dreams. She had never shared her dreams or daydreams with anyone except Clay and she wondered how Leonard would respond. She recalled that he had looked up, smiled, and said something she had never forgotten.

"Remember this, Morgan," Leonard had said, "imagery spawned by imagination is the dialectic of the unconscious. There are those whose imaginative faculties are so advanced as to allow them to extract and distill the essence of what their imaginations call forth. All matter of things that our minds can imagine exist somewhere in our mysterious universe. Think of our universe as a large unseen department store where we can go and select anything we want, limited only by the extent of our imaginations. Once we have made our selections and using our the power of imagery, we can begin the process of assimilation-creating whatever gives us a sense of satisfaction and fulfillment. For those who are sufficiently advanced in the art of imagery, there are no limits to what may be accomplished. Teleportation, for example; a person can leave their bodies, travel through time and space and, if they wish, be seen in two places at the same time. A growing number of people are using imagery to heal themselves mentally, physically and spiritually, but what is not widely known is that in certain instances where peace and harmony are the principal desires, there are those who are capable of disappearing into their creations either for a short period of time or forever."

Leonard's words had carried a somewhat inscrutable, but nevertheless compelling and comforting cerebration unlike his comfortless and all too accurate prediction that her years at Centre might be met with friendless courtesies and stinging criticism if she were to incorporate such thinking in her classes on Speculative Religions. Her students, she had found, had welcomed Leonard's beliefs and debated their virtue with a fierceness and passion not seen or felt in her department since her arrival. On the other hand, many of her colleagues both in and outside her department, had looked upon her courses with haughty disdain and resentment. They had characterized the content of her courses as fanciful and lacking in academic merit. The atmosphere had become so inflamed that on several occasions her scholarship had been called into question. Leonard, she thought, had been right when he said her department gave the impression of encouraging individuality, but succeeded in creating only sameness.

Leonard had, she remembered, announced to the faculty at their year end meeting this past May that at the age of 72, he was retiring after 38 years at Centre.

She smiled as she remembered how she had studied him from across the room and how her jaw ached from watching him bite on his meerschaum. She wondered if the cherry scented smoke stung his eyes. As if tapped on his shoulder by some unseen hand, Leonard had turned to see her watching him and, nodding an acknowledgment, weaved his way through the milling and chattering crowd toward her.

"My dear Morgan," he had said, throwing out his hands, one of which was holding a dangerously wobbling cup of tea, "of all these people I'm going to miss you the most."

Morgan, over the years, had come to appreciate his expressive greetings and his friendly casualness.

"I'm going to miss you too, Leonard," she remembered saying.

Although she had been preparing herself for that evening and steeling herself against any show of tearful emotion, she felt a tear form, which Leonard's thumb gently wiped from her cheek. Guiding her to a less crowded and out of the way corner of the student union, Crawford had set down his cup and taken both her hands in his.

"Our time together has been well spent," he had half whispered. "Remember the mythical Sisyphus who was compelled to roll a stone to the top of a hill, but found that as he neared the top, he would lose his grip and the stone would roll back down the hill again? Many of our colleagues here are like Sisyphus. The more they know, the more they don't know. It's one of the laws of diminishing returns. The philosopher Kant once said that he awakened at five in the morning not to think as other people think. Unfortunately, most people awaken at six and seven and even at nine and ten and think as others do. You, my dear Morgan, are not one of them. You are one of us."

She had been struck by both his words and his tone and she recalled that her question as to what he had meant by "one of us" had gone unanswered. He had, however, told her that she had learned her lessons well and that she possessed the power to make her dreams come true. He had ended their last meeting by telling her that he was leaving for England shortly and that their paths would cross again soon.

The sudden ring of the doorbell broke the spell and sent Morgan bounding to the front door, the quilt, caught on a skirt button, dragging after her. Standing in the doorway, his raincoat stained with rain, his black hair matted to his head, her husband, looking somewhat forlorn, stood with his arms encircling two huge bags of groceries.

"Honey, I'm home," he said, half laughing and giving her one of those 'have I been gone too long?' looks.

Unmindful of what he so precariously balanced, Morgan threw her arms around his neck and kissed him on both cheeks.

"Have you missed me?" he asked, while struggling to set one of the thoroughly wet bags down.

"Have I missed you? Have I missed you? You leave me here for two hours in a house that reeks of mystery and you ask if I missed you? If and when we need groceries again I'm going with you. I don't want to be left alone in this house again." Although Morgan had half laughed when she said it, he detected a note of finality in her voice.

"Did something happen while I was gone?" Clay asked, placing one of the bags down on the kitchen table and going back to the hall to retrieve the second.

"Yes something happened," Morgan replied, carefully examining the contents of the bags. "What took you so long? I thought the grocer was just down the street. It didn't take you two hours to get these two bags of groceries."

"Let me get this wet raincoat off and I'll tell you about it," Clay called from the hall.

"It's chilly in here," Clay said as he returned, looking comfortable in his flannel robe. Orange and blue flames licked the two logs that he placed on the fire and the room took on a warm and cozy look once again.

"Now tell me what happened," Clay said, taking her hand and moving his chair so that it faced hers.

"I thought I heard someone call the name Duncan Allister from somewhere in the house," Morgan said, giving Clay a troubled glance. "I don't know if I had dozed or what, but I distinctly heard someone call out the name."

"Who's Duncan Allister?" Clay asked, reaching over and giving the logs a poke with the fireplace iron.

"He was the founder of Centre College and I believe Leonard said that he had served as ambassador to the Court of St. James under President Grant." Picking up her cup, Morgan took a sip of tea which by this time was ice cold, but she didn't seem to notice.

"Now tell me about the grocer," Morgan said, in an abrupt change of subject.

"The grocer's name is Charcross and he and his wife, Helen, have operated this store, certainly not like one of our supermarkets, for the past 35 years," Clay said, moving his chair closer to Morgan. He took the cold cup of tea from her and placed it on a chairside table.

"I asked him about this cottage and he said that as long as he could remember, the cottage had but a few occupants who didn't seem to stay very long. He knows Alan, and they agree that it's customary for a couple to move in, stay a week or a month, and then move out. No one seemed to know why, and of course, he said it wasn't long before people were saying that it was haunted. School children and other passersby, he said, have claimed to have seen faces in the window and some parents will not let their children walk past the cottage on this side of the road for fear that they will be taken or that something horrible will befall them."

"Was his wife there?" Morgan asked, studying Clay's face for a sign that he believed what he had heard.

"Yes, she came out of the back room as we were talking and said that one morning about five years ago, when she opened for business, she found a note taped to the door asking if someone could deliver the grocery items that were listed on the piece of paper. Her husband was busy so she drove them over. She knocked and when a women answered, she asked who she was speaking to and the woman said Mrs. Simmons. She said she had no chance to look around the house, but said it seemed quiet enough."

"Did you ask her what Mrs. Simmons looked like?" Morgan asked, looking down at her hands.

"Yes, she said the best she could recall, she was a short buxom woman, with a round face and hair pulled back into a pug. She said she had a kindly face and smiling eyes, and that she had paid handsomely for the delivery."

"That's all?" Morgan hoped that there would be more.

"That's all honey, but we now know Mrs. Simmons actually exists. Oh, she did say that the grocery list contained the word Hyssop, but she didn't know what it meant and her husband didn't know either."

"Hyssop, hyssop," Morgan repeated the word as a statement rather than a question.

"Do you know what it means?" Clay asked anxiously.

"Yes, it's an herb that was used by the ancients in rites of purification," Morgan replied through pursed lips.

The room grew silent; the only sound was the popping

and crackling of the fire and the rain drumming against the windows.

"The wind is up," Clay said somewhat absently, "I imagine we'll hear alot of creaks in this old house tonight." He again poked the logs, sending a shower of sparks up the chimney.

Throughout Clay's absence, Morgan had reminded herself again and again that there was no earthly reason why she should be afraid in such a lovely, cozy cottage. Clay would certainly be gone again on some errand leaving her alone. After all, she had told herself, she had not seen anything frightening—only the sounds. The sounds, had she heard them or did she imagine them? Several moments would pass in silence before she would pose the question she so badly wanted to ask all day.

"Honey," she began hesitantly, her eyes riveted on the fire as she spoke, "did you hear a woman's laugher and a sound like the front door being opened last night? I didn't sleep well, you know I never do the first night in a strange place, but I swear I heard the front door open. It has that funny little squeak. I didn't hear any footsteps, but I know I heard the door open."

Clay, who had gotten up and disappeared before she had finished, reappeared with two cups of steaming tea in his hands.

"You may have heard something, honey," he said, placing the cup down beside her and giving her an anxious look. "But what you heard couldn't have been the front door opening. I double locked it before we went to bed. One of the locks is a dead bolt. I'm sorry, I was probably fast asleep before my head hit the pillow."

For a moment, the room grew silent. Clay noticed that Morgan's hand shivered as she sipped her tea. Her eyes, he thought, cast in the light of the dancing flames, had taken on a haunting and faraway look.

Chapter 3

The Box

Henley Street in Stratford was crowded with market day shoppers. The lowering clouds and rain of the past several days had moved to the east and a bright afternoon sun shown through strands of high whispy clouds.

Life at the cottage for Morgan and Clay had begun to take on a settled feeling and, except for the expected creaks and thumps, they had experienced no further unexplained disturbances. Early in the morning, with the back of the cottage bathed in a weak, but welcome sun, Clay and Morgan had taken their customary stroll down to the river followed by a dozen waddling, quacking, hungry ducks.

The unruffled surface of the Avon sparkled in the morning sun as if inlaid with thousands of diamonds, and two white swans, knowing that food was at hand, signaled their morning greeting by circling and dipping their heads in the water.

"Isn't it beautiful?" Morgan said, putting her arm through Clay's and placing her head on his shoulder. "It's hard to imagine a more serene scene."

Clay, who had been casting bread on the water, looked down at her and smiled. As they strolled arm in arm toward the rear of the cottage, the memory of walking with her uncle on the soft dewy lawn in back of their house in

Fincastle on a similar bright sun splashed morning flashed through her mind. They had been talking about dreams and her uncle had said ever so quietly, "Wherever you go or whatever you do, Morgan, remember that dreams are the windows of heaven." It was odd, she thought, shrugging her shoulders why she should recall bits of her uncle's conversation that occurred over 25 years ago.

Clay felt her shoulders lift. "What are you thinking about?" he asked, giving Morgan an inquiring look. "Did I lose you for a moment?"

"No, I was thinking about what my uncle had said about dreams. I'll tell you later, but first I must get a picture of the river and the back of the cottage. Now if you'll back up a bit, I'll get you with the cottage and then you can take one of me by the river. It's the last two on the roll and we can take them in to get them developed when we go into Stratford later this morning."

Although they had hoped to leave the cottage by mid morning and after getting hoplessly lost on streets whose names seemed to suddenly change at each intersection, it was early afternoon before they arrived at Wood Street in downtown Stratford.

"Did you ever think that someday you would be walking in the footsteps of the world's most famous playwright?" Morgan asked, slipping her arm through his as they walked past picturesque cottage type shops and beautifully-preserved half timbered buildings. "What was that line from the *Merchant of Venice?* 'from the ends of the world they come to kiss this shrine...' well something like that."

"I've always found Shakespeare's plays a bit incomprehensible," Clay said, giving Morgan a look of exaggerated disdain.

"You do not," Morgan returned, giving Clay a look of mock annoyance. "We have been to a half dozen of his plays and you said you enjoyed them as much as I."

"Well..." Clay didn't finish.

An elderly gentleman wearing a belted hunting jacket and knickers who had been walking beside them touched Clay's arm lightly.

"Sorry," he said, giving Clay and Morgan a shy smile, "but I couldn't help overhearing your comments about the Bard of Avon. I would agree with you young man that the language is a bit bewildering at times, but I have found that closing my eyes occasionally and listening to what is being said somehow improves my understanding of the play's meaning and accompanying subtleties. Well Cheerio." Tipping his cap, he was off down the street.

"Well that was interesting," Morgan said, giving Clay an amusing smile.

"Hardly accidental," Clay retuned laconically.

After a leisurely lunch in a cozy bakery whose windows displayed neat rows of delicious pastries, Morgan and Clay decided to separate with the reminder that they would meet again at the corner of High and Sheep Streets at around four. Clay kissed her cheek and disappeared down the crowded street in search of a English-looking flat cap and an ascot to go with the flannel robe that Morgan had given him for his thirty-seventh birthday.

Morgan had first intended to shop for a moss green pocket cape and a wool lap blanket, but then decided that she would first spend a half hour or so at the Public Records Office seeing if she could find a reference to one John Barnett.

She filled in the name on a light blue card and handed it to a short balding man who stood behind a shoulder high counter.

"John Barnett, John Barnett," he repeated. "My name is Barnet but I spell it with one T," he said, peering at her over rectangular shaped spectacles.

"Is it a common name in this area?" Morgan asked, eyeing the man with increased interest.

"It is in Warwickshire," he replied, giving Morgan a pleasant smile. "Sometimes the names are spelled with one and sometimes with two Ts, but I believe we probably came from a common set of ancestors. If we are related we go back a long way. I found that a Clarence Barnet spelled with one T was listed in the Domesday Book which William the Conquerer ordered compiled in 1086."

"Do you think you might have some record of a John Barnett?" Morgan asked, trying hard not to show her rising excitement. "I was told by my uncle, who has spent years tracking our ancestors in the States, that he had lived in or around Stratford, but had emigrated to the Virginia Colony in the early 1700's. However, we seemed to have lost him. There is no record of him on the early census or church rolls. He seems to have disappeared."

"That's not suprising given how primitive the country was and some claim still is," the man said, giving Morgan a wry smile. "I suspected you were an American. Come round the side of the counter and sit at this desk and I'll see what I might find. Bye the bye, my name is Donald...and yours?"

"Morgan Barnett Ashton, with two Ts."

Since Morgan's arrival, the small waiting area had become crowded and after a long half hour of hearing the office staff repeat "Can I help you?" Donald reappeared, carrying a thick leather-bound ledger which he said contained the names of a number of Barnetts spelled with two Ts. Pulling a wooden chair up close to hers, he dropped the heavy ledger down on the desk with a resounding thud.

"This is interesting," he said, opening the ledger to a mark. "This section contains the names of members of a fraternity called the Guild of the Silver Cross. The guild I'm told came into existence around 1250, and you will notice," he said tracing his finger down the page "that a John Barnett is listed among the members up to the time it was dissolved by order of the King in the mid 1700's."

"What was the purpose of the guild?" Morgan asked, running her own finger down the list of badly faded names.

"Guild members, we believe, devoted considerable attention to assisting the poor and infirm, but letters that have remained in the hands of descendants seem to indicate that the guild's fundamental mission was to free the mind from its prison-like condition."

"Free the mind?" Morgan asked, looking up suddenly. Her eyes narrowed.

"Well, yes," Donald continued, polishing his spectacles with a pale blue, monogrammed handkerchief. "Their writings are filled with references to dreams and waking dreamstates. Interestingly, several letters that I have been shown tell of experiments by guild members to hold onto their dream memory as long as they wished. In doing so, according to these writings, members were able to pass into other realms, leaving no trace of their passing."

"We have no answers to the rapid memory loss of dreams," Morgan interjected. Ten minutes or so is about the limit of our waking memories. Do the letters tell how members were able to sustain their memories?" Morgan asked without looking up.

"The letters are silent on that subject, but during the witch trials in the 17th century, guild leaders were accused of practicing sorcery and they, as well as guild members, were branded as sorcerers. Some were burned at the stake and some were hung. Others went underground, so to speak, or escaped to the colonies as I suspect your relative did."

Morgan felt her heart beat a little faster. "I wonder if this is him?" Morgan asked, pointing to a name half way down the yellowed page.

"For their time, the secretaries of the guild kept meticulous records of the members. What does it say?" Donald asked, looking up sharply.

"It says that John Clarence Barnett, born in 1662,

became a member of the Guild on his 20th birthday. It lists him as a farmer and schoolmaster. In 1694, he was elected Master of the Guild. I wonder what master means; do you know Donald?"

"No I don't, Mrs. Ashton." There was a noticeable hesitation in his reply that made Morgan think that he did.

Glancing at her watch, she was somewhat startled to see that two hours had passed so rapidly. She quickly scribbled down the information that she had read and closed the ledger.

"Thank you, Donald," she said, holding our her hand. "You've been grand, but how did you know where to find this particular ledger? There must be hundreds of them back there in the vault?"

Donald took her hand and their eyes met. 'His eyes are almost almond-like and transparent', Morgan thought as he saw her to the door.

"I was glad to be of service, Mrs. Ashton, and I hope you'll visit us again. These old records are wonderful windows to our past and sometimes to our present and future."

The lighting in the office had been poor and the sudden entrance into bright sun hurt her eyes as she hurried down Henley Street to her rendezvous with Clay. She was already 15 minutes late and she hoped that Clay didn't think she had gotten lost. As she circled the roundabout from Henley onto High Street, she thought she heard a voice call her name. She continued to walk, but she heard her name called again. This time there was no mistaking it. She turned and saw Alan Crabtree hurrying after her.

"I'm so glad to see you, Mrs. Ashton," Alan said, tipping his cap. His face was slightly pink and he sounded a trifle winded. "It's market day today and the missus and me stock our cupboards for the whole week."

"Could we talk while we walk?" Morgan asked, looking

at her watch. "I promised to meet Clay near here at four and it's now close to 4:15."

"No, I don't mind a bit. But I 'ave a post from Mrs. Simmons addressed to you and Mr. Ashton and I thought if I could catch up with you it would save me a walk over later."

"A letter from Mrs. Simmons, well that's interesting." Morgan slowed, giving Alan a suprised look. How extraordinary, she thought, that Alan would find her on such a crowded street.

"Yes, it arrived this morning and as you can see, the postmark says it comes from Morning Meadow," Alan replied, giving her a vague smile.

Rounding the corner from High onto Sheep Street, they literally bumped into Clay, who was standing with his back flattened against a shop window worriedly scanning the crowds for some sign of a familiar face.

"Sorry I'm late, honey," Morgan said, reaching up and giving Clay a peck on his cheek. "I had the most interesting visit at the Public Records Office, but I'll tell you about it later."

"Alan, it's nice to see you again," Clay said, returning his wife's kiss and gripping Alan's hand in a friendly handshake.

"It's nice to see both of you," Alan said, tipping his cap, his face bathed in a wide grin. "I was telling my missus that we 'aven't 'eard from Mrs. Simmons, so I don't know if there will be new people at the cottage after you leave. Usually years can go by before someone else moves in, but then comes this post addressed to you and Mrs. Ashton."

"Yes, Alan chased me down to give me this," Morgan said, producing the letter from her raincoat pocket.

Clay glanced at it briefly, but Morgan could tell that the pub across the street had for the moment captured his interest far more than the letter.

"Maybe she's asking us to stay another week," he said, giving Morgan a grimacing look, "but first let's have a drink in that very English-looking pub over there and talk about it. Alan, we'd be happy if you would join us."

"Yes Alan, won't you join us? Morgan agreed. "There may be something in the letter that you need to know."

"Market day usually leaves me with a powerful thirst and I'd be 'appy to join you," Alan said, touching Morgan's arm, "but my missus says that if she has to carry those heavy market baskets to the car again she'd take a switch to me."

"I know what you mean," Clay said, winking and gripping Alan's hand in parting handshake. "We'll be leaving sometime tomorrow for Oxford, but we'll stop in and say goodbye."

"Come in the mornin' if you can," Alan said, and with a wave, he disappeared up the street.

"I want to show you what I bought," Clay said as they were comfortably seated in a booth alongside a low and slowly burning fire.

Plunging his hand into a dark green bag, he proudly presented a navy and green plaid cap which he proceeded to place on his head with an air of expected acceptance. Morgan,who had been studying the menu, looked up to see her husband tugging at the visor. Every time he did, the back of the cap would raise up along with the bill.

With Clay eyeing her with a questioning mixture of hope and dark suspicion, Morgan knew that she would have to be careful about how she should respond to his unattractive and undersized purchase that looked, she thought, like a pancake sitting rakishly atop his head.

"Honey," she began, but couldn't finish. She couldn't contain herself and her smile suddenly dissolved into a burst of laughter. Clay, intent on making the cap fit to the point of stretching it, tried hard to ignore his wife's ticklish response.

"Clay I'm sorry, but the cap is much too small. You either need a smaller head or a bigger cap. I'll go with you and we'll find one, I promise."

She gently removed the cap and placed it on the table alongside the letter. It was then that they both noticed that the envelope carried the distinct smell of lilac.

The two hours that they spent eating and sampling several varieties of English and Irish ales passed quickly. Morgan had recounted her discoveries at the Public Records Office and Clay had told her about a chance meeting he had with a little old man who described in great detail how the buildings shook and the doors and windows rattled in Stratford the night of November 14, 1940, when Nazi bombers nearly destroyed Coventry.

"Were ye here, lad?" he had asked Clay. Clay said he wasn't. He hadn't been born and that he was an American. The old man smiled and patting him on the shoulder ambled off. His parting words were, "God bless America and President Roosevelt."

"Let's open the letter," Morgan said, sipping the last of her ale. "I'm dying to know what's in it. Maybe she wants us to visit her in Morning Meadow. I've read that the standing stones there predate those at Stonehenge."

She handed her nail file to Clay, who carefully slit the envelope, taking care not to harm the return address neatly penned on the back flap.

"I love the smell of lilac," Morgan said, taking the envelope and pressing it against her cheek. "Let me join you on your side and we'll read it together."

Dear Mr. and Mrs. Ashton:

Hope your stay at our cottage has been a pleasant one. We call the cottage the Odyssey because for many of our guests it is a place to rest before they embark on an adventure like no other. En-

gland, as you may have already learned, is a supreme adventure. There are many places of mystery and magic in our land and I suspect your research into our most ancient and primitive religions, Mrs. Ashton, will be both fulfilling and rewarding.

The purpose of my letter is to seek a favor. In the bottom right hand desk drawer in the study you will find a black lacquered box with two half moons inlaid in pearl on the cover. It's my understanding that your research will take you to the earthworks and the stone circles of our Morning Meadow. It would be a pleasure to welcome you to our village and to my home, and I would be very appreciative if you would bring the box with you. In the event that I may be away on holiday when you arrive, please leave the box at the home of Mr. Nigel Wittlewaite who lives next door.

With Cordial regards
Mrs. Claire Simmons

"Did you see a black box in the desk drawer?" Clay asked, placing the letter back in the envelope.

"No, I never looked in the drawers, but how did she know we would be visiting Morning Meadow?"

"Cheerio probably told her," Clay said, getting up and placing the much maligned cap on Morgan's head. "We'd better get your film to a camera store before they close. Besides, the light is failing and I'm not sure I'd be able to find our way back to the cottage after dark."

The clouds of the past two days had reappeared and a misty rain was falling as they turned into the lane that led to their cottage.

"Did you leave a light burning in the study?" Morgan asked, somewhat hesitantly as their car came to a crunching stop on the gravel driveway. The lamp perched upon a post in the yard bathed the cottage in an eerie white light.

"No, I don't think so," Clay replied, retrieving his purchase from the back seat. "Maybe Mrs. Simmons has a timer set to go on after dark and we haven't noticed it before because the study lamp always been on."

"I wonder," Morgan half whispered to herself. The cottage felt chill and clammy.

"Thank God for central heating," Clay said, turning up the thermostat. "I'd hate having to make a fire every time we wanted to warm these old walls."

Morgan didn't reply, but threw her raincoat on a chair near the door and quickly walked to the desk. Resting in the lower right hand drawer was the black lacquered box. Morgan's hand trembled slightly as she removed it and placed it on the desk. Inside was a quartz crystal shaped in the form of a scarab attached to a long gold chain. The smooth colorless crystal rested on a bed of soft black velvet.

Clay, carrying two small glasses of sherry, gave his wife an amused smile as he appeared in the doorway and caught sight of the box.

"What did you find, honey?" he said, peering over his glass of sherry he was sipping. Their eyes met briefly as he placed her glass on the desk beside her.

"I found this," Morgan said as she gently extracted the crystal, holding it up by its long, delicately-crafted chain. "Isn't it beautiful? See, there's a card attached to the underside of the cover."

"It looks like a beetle," Clay's face registered a mixture of suprise and interest as he stretched out his hand to examine the crystal more closely. "It feels warm to the touch."

"Hold it by the chain," Morgan directed. "The energy in the crystal belongs to someone and if someone else touches it there is a danger of mixing magnetisms, which can reduce its power. Crystals operate like radio receivers. People use them for a variety of reasons. Some say crystals protect them from the power of unseen forces, others use them for divination and still others say crystals allow them to communicate with the spirit world."

"Do crystals usually come in the shape of a beetle?" Clay asked, his face bathed in an exaggerated frown. "I've never seen a crystal beetle."

"The beetle... now Clay be serious, the beetle..." She couldn't finish. She knew that whenever Clay detected that his question would produce an expansive reply, he would begin to smile-a smile which he knew would destroy her chain of thought and make her laugh. Her laughter seemed always to signal a change of subject.

"I'm sorry, honey," Clay said, giving her a sobering and penitent look. "What were you saying about the beetle or scarab?"

"I was about to say, before you so shamelessly interrupted me, that the beetle was looked upon by the ancient Egyptians as having magical and mystical powers. They wore carvings of the beetle around their necks as protective ornaments and they were buried with them to insure their entry into an afterlife."

"What's the card say?" Clay took a sip of his sherry and studied his wife, who had removed the card from the cover and was examining it intently.

"It's in French," Morgan said, looking up. *Ill est temps de rentrer* .

"Can you translate? What do you think it means?" Clay took the card, looked at it for a moment, and then handed it back.

"My French is terribly rusty , but I recognize the words home and return. I don't know what it means."

The sudden ring of the telephone startled them both. "I'll get it, honey," Clay said, retrieving his drink and disappearing into the kitchen.

Morgan sat, tracing the moon-shaped inlays on the box with her finger. 'This old house,' she thought, is filled with brooding secrets. 'I'll be glad when we leave here tomorrow.'

Almost absently, she glanced at the picture over the fireplace. Her fascination with the painting was evident in her eyes.

"I wonder," she said half out loud "who those people in the painting are?"

Alan's parting comment about how the people in the painting looked familiar sent a chill deep within her.

"It's Theopholis Weeks," Clay called from the kitchen. "He wants to know when we'll be arriving in Oxford. Do you want to talk to him?"

Her hands felt cold as she took the receiver. "It's so nice of you to call, Professor Weeks." She was aware that her voice sounded slightly unsteady. "We'll be leaving Stratford tomorrow morning and we should arrive in Oxford sometime on Monday. We so look forward to meeting you."

"If I can take the liberty to call you Morgan, Mrs. Ashton, then I'll answer to Theo, the name most of the people around this ancient pile are most familiar with." Noting the slight waver in Morgan's voice, Theo paused and then continued. "Is there something wrong, Mrs. Ashton? You haven't contracted a cold have you? Many Americans who come to England for study this time of year spend most of their time wiping their noses and ingesting gallons of cold medicines."

"No, nothing is wrong, Theo, its just that on occasion, this cottage seems a bit glacial," Morgan replied, trying hard to sound convincing.

"You don't have a ghost on the premises?" Theo asked, emitting what sounded like a half laugh. "Ghosts are household ornaments in many old cottages in England, you know.

They often show complete disdain for the comforts of the occupants and on occasion, they can become overly expressive."

"I'm not sure whether we have a ghost or not, but if we do, we haven't been able to discover its motives," Morgan said, giving Clay, who was standing beside her, a sidelong glance.

"If convenient," Theo continued, "I have made arrangements for you and Clay to see a cottage on Chestnut Lane that I think will meet your needs while you're here. I will be in my office at New College in the afternoons between two and four. With that I'm afraid I have to ring off. I have students waiting for me whose general unreliability of keeping precise appointments is a matter of grave annoyance to me. Goodnight to you both."

"Good night Theo."

Morgan turned to look at Clay, who was pouring himself another sherry.

"Want one?" he asked, raising his half filled glass.

"I think we will find our Professor Weeks a delight," Morgan said somewhat absently as she looked beyond Clay into the dark yard.

It was then that she heard the name Duncan Alister being called again, clear and distinct. She wasn't dreaming and, like before, the voice seemed to come from deep within the house. Clay noticed her sudden shudder.

"Are you cold, honey?" Clay asked, giving Morgan a concerned frown.

He hadn't heard the voice, Morgan said to herself, her gaze straying briefly to Clay's face. Why...why am I hearing these sounds and he doesn't? It's no accident that we're here is it? Her thoughts were shifting rapidly. No, not an accident. The cottage had somehow beckoned them, but why?

She felt her heart pound furiously as she turned again to

face Clay. She could not retrain herself any longer; she must know. "Did you hear it, did you hear someone call out just now? Please, please Clay, tell me if you heard it." Morgan implored through quivering lips.

Startled by her sudden fear and near panic, Clay put his arms around her shoulders.

"Honey I didn't hear..."

Morgan's frightened, imploring look stopped him. Clay's tight embrace could not stop her from shaking. All color had drained from her face and her hazel eyes seemed filled with a strange irridescent glow. Clay took Morgan's face in his cupped hands and kissed her. They stood silent and motionless for a long moment.

"You were right, honey," Clay whispered. "This house does hold many secrets. We'll pack tonight and leave by first light in the morning."

Chapter 4

The Ruins

The grass and trees were wet with dew and glistened under a brilliant sun on October 20, when Morgan and Clay said goodbye to their cottage.

Although Clay had missed their road leading off a roundabout at Chipping Norton and had strayed into a line of oncoming traffic, the trip between Stratford and Burford had been quietly uneventful. For much of the drive, Morgan had stared glassidly out the side window seemingly oblivious to the passing landscape. The sudden swerving and the blaring of horns had jolted her out of her thoughtful silence.

"I'm sorry, honey," she said, giving him a wistful smile and placing her hand on his arm. "I haven't been very good company. Where are we?"

"We're a few miles from Burford. Were you dozing?"

"No I keep thinking about the voice I heard last night. Clay, I can't believe you didn't hear it."

"Was it a man or woman's voice?" Clay asked, somewhat awkwardly. He could not disbelieve what Morgan said she had heard, but neither could he affirm it.

"It was a woman's. It wasn't hideous or ghastly, but the suddenness of it...it sounded like it came from everywhere, yet, nowhere. Clay, it frightened me terribly."

"I know it did," Clay said, giving her a sidelong glance, "but that's all behind us."

"I wonder if it is," Morgan said to herself. Her gaze strayed briefly to a flock of sheep that were grazing on a roadside hill. The rolling hills were not unlike the landscape around Fincastle and the farmhouse they passed reminded her of her aunt and uncle's rusty red brick house with its white trim and bullseye glass windows that looked out over the ruins of a house of a prominent Fincastle family that had been destroyed by fire over a hundred years ago. She shivered just a bit as she recalled lying on her bed one moonlit summer night, her head cupped in her hands looking out at the ruins and wondering what it must have been like living in such elegant surroundings. Memories of that evening seemed as fresh as the night she experienced them. She remembered closing her eyes for a moment and when she opened them, the ruins had been transformed into a beautiful mansion ablaze with lights. The air was filled with laughter and music, and a shiny, black coach pulled by two beautiful white horses had stopped in front of the columned porch. When she closed her eyes and opened them again, the shrub covered ruins had appeared, looking desolate and forlorn under the pale light of the moon. She remembered mentioning her experience to her uncle who, after studying her for a long moment, said something she thought quite odd.

"Events that impress one's memory as a child or as a young person will never be eliminated by age or education. You have a gift, my dear Morgan, a gift that the Scotch called fey. It will call you from time to time, seeking your attention. Be sure to seek a companion who will share your gift as well as your excursions."

Deep in thought, Morgan had not heard Clay speak, but saw his questioning look.

"Honey...honey," he persisted, giving her an amusing smile, "I hate to interrupt your cerebrations, but could you reach back and find our thermos? I could use a cup of coffee."

Fortunately, traffic on A361 between Chipping Norton and Burford had not been heavy. Although their driving excursions around Stratford had remained accident-free, much of the car's controls seemed to defy all attempts at understanding and the act of driving on the right side continued to produce for Clay a feeling of irrestible dread.

Noticing that both his hands were firmly locked on the steering wheel, Morgan raised the cup to his lips. "Clay, have you ever felt completely at home in a place that you had never been before?"

"Once," Clay said, turning and nodding. "My parents took us boys on a trip east one year and we stopped to visit my mother's Mennonite relatives around Lancaster, Pennsylvania. Yes, I had the distinct feeling that I had been there before. I love the area and yes, it felt like home."

They were traversing a broad valley bordered by gently-sloping, treeless hills dotted here and there by scores of grazing sheep. Ancient stone walls and ruler-straight hedges separated endless pastures, still carpeted in a lush green. And every now and again they would pass a tree-canopied lane that led to cozy-looking farm houses nestled in the folds of a field or a flat, steepled, stone church festooned in a mantle of blood-red ivy.

"Clay, I..." Morgan didn't finish. Traffic had gotten heavier and the blue roundabout sign with its puzzling set of white arrows and unfamiliar names had appeared all too quickly.

"Damn. I think we missed the road to Oxford." The muscles in Clay's face tightened. "I should have gone half way around and then straight ahead. Now we're going south. Did you get the names and numbers on that board? We'll find a place to turn around and go back."

"No, let's see where this road leads us," Morgan said, giving Clay a sly smile and taking a sip of the coffee she was gingerly cradling in both hands. "Maybe it will lead to one of those wonderfully quaint English villages that we've read about."

They had travelled several miles before they met another car and Clay had relaxed to where he felt comfortable in holding the coffee cup himself. The narrow, unfrequented road seemed to parallel a placid and mirror-like stream that would disappear from time to time amidst water meadows shimmering in the afternoon sun.

They had passed several steepled churches around whose time-mellowed walls huddled quaint, honey colored, thatched cottages whose windows were shaded by white lace curtains. Their doors were colorfully painted in shades of mustard yellow, forest green, and dark maroon.

"I love it," Morgan said somewhat absently. "This is how I remembered England to be."

"Remembered?" Clay asked, giving her a suprised look. "That's interesting."

"No, honey, remembered isn't the right word. It's just that this is what I wanted England to be. Clay, let's not go on to Oxford today. Let's have a picnic with the food we brought and stay in one of these villages. Maybe we can find a hotel or a bed and breakfast."

A small rectangular sign announced that Minster Swallow Falls lay off the highway to the right. After several turns, Clay pulled up in front of a two-story, straw-colored stone building capped by a slate roof that had blackened with age and was covered by tufts of green lichen. Lace curtains covered the ten small-paned windows that overlooked the road, and above the entrance a signboard displayed the painting of a white swan.

"What a wonderful discovery," Morgan said as she led Clay through the low doorway that opened into a cozy sitting room where a fire was burning brightly in a large, rock fireplace.

The faint, but acrid smell of wood smoke mixed with the

scent of furniture polish filled the room. They stood for a moment surveying their surroundings when an unseen voice called, "Can I help you?" from a side room, followed by the sound of a glass shattering on the flagstone floor.

Through an arched doorway, a short man with carrot-colored hair appeared carrying a bar towel in one hand and a broom and a dustpan in the other.

"I'm sorry if the noise startled you," he said, peering over wire-rimed spectacles that sat precariously close to the end of his nose. "I've asked the management to use plastic water glasses instead of glass; its the floor you know, but they won't hear of it."

"Yes," Morgan agreed, eyeing the man with amused interest. "We'd like a room for tonight. I take it this is a hotel?"

"Oh yes ma'am, guests have been staying here since before Columbus discovered your country. There have been a few improvements, like plumbing and heating and such, but otherwise, little has changed."

"How did you know we were Americans?" Clay asked, walking over to the fireplace for a closer look at its construction.

"Oh, it's not difficult. By the way, my name is Oswald Mayberry. Americans who come here usually stand for some minutes studying the surroundings as you did. As you can tell, our ceilings are low and we had one American, quite tall, who bumped his head on one of the beams. Not terribly happy I can tell you. The half plaster and half wood walls I'm told are original to the hotel. I imagine you don't have anything quite so old in your country. We English are so used to living with centuries-old buildings and furnishings that we don't give them a second thought."

"We'd like to register," Morgan said, motioning Clay to join her. "We haven't eaten since early morning and I'm starved."

"Well ma'am, we won't be serving dinner until seven and our cook doesn't come to work until six, but I'll see if I can discover a bit of refreshment in the cooler."

"Thank you, Oswald," Clay said, turning toward the door, "but we have a bulging picnic basket in the car. Honey, why don't you register and I'll start bringing in our luggage. Maybe Oswald can tell you where we can hold our picnic. By the way, what's the name of the stream that runs by the hotel?"

"It's the Windrush, sir, and a beautiful little river it is. It rises in the Cotswolds and joins the Thames just south of here."

"Are there falls on the river near here?" Morgan asked as she surveyed the names on the leather-bound register.

"No, there are no falls on the Windrush near here. I have no idea why the name was added to our village, but we do have an abundance of swallows as you no doubt will see on your picnic. Keep your basket covered."

Oswald's instructions were to follow the narrow footpath that began in the rear of the inn. "It meanders through a grove of beech trees," he said with determined cheerfulness, "but with persistence it will lead you to a spot where you can enjoy yourselves, undisturbed by noisy traffic."

"Oswald was right. What a wonderful spot for a picnic," Morgan said, spreading a large red and black plaid blanket on the ground.

The blanket lay but a few feet from the glimmering surface of the slow-moving Windrush. The grass and nearby wild flowers had not lost their midsummer luster, and several nearby trees gave their surroundings a dappled and inviting appearance.

"Did Oswald say what those ruined buildings were over there?" Clay asked while examining the contents of the slatted picnic basket. "By the thickness of the walls, they look like they may have been part of a small castle or maybe a church."

"No, he didn't," Morgan replied, giving Clay a mildly suprised look. "I wonder why he didn't. We can ask him when we get back."

The shadows were beginning to lengthen as Morgan and Clay consumed the last of their four ham sandwiches and two very tasty strawberry tarts. The two thermos' had dispensed the last drop of coffee and except for the tantalizing singing of a brownish bird that Morgan thought was a skylark, the afternoon had been serenely quiet.

Once, and briefly, a woman dressed in a hat and tweed suit appeared leading a group of children through the ruins, but it was evident that her charges were more interested in horseplay than historical snooping and they soon trooped off.

Morgan and Clay lay facing each other, the blanket stretched beneath them. Clay, with one hand propped under his head, drew his finger across Morgan's forehead, down the sides of her cheeks and under her chin. He fixed her with a thoughtful gaze.

"You are beautiful you know," he whispered.

Her long, flaxen-colored hair fell softly, partially covering her cheeks and curling slightly under her chin, giving her face, he thought, a cameo-like appearance. Her lips were full, her skin smooth and devoid of makeup. Especially striking were her eyes. There was a searching quality about her eyes and although pale blue, they seemed to Clay to change color with the light. For the moment, they seemed almost black.

With her forefinger pressed against her lower lip, Morgan returned Clay's stready gase with a look of wistful affection. Her cheeks reddened, as they always did when someone paid her an unexpected compliment.

"I wonder what we'll find in Oxford," Clay said, suddenly rolling over on his back and watching several fork-tailed swallows swoop and turn above the nearby trees. "I picture Theopholis Weeks as a Barry Fitzgerald type of character—small, with a wrinkled face and squinting eyes."

"I don't picture him that way at all," Morgan said, somewhat absently as she raised herself to a half-sitting position and stared at the ruins as if something had suddenly caught her attention. "I see him as being tall, balding, sharp eyed, thin, almost frail, and with a Van Dyke beard.

Morgan caught her breath. A woman wearing a long, dark grey dress, her face the color of milk, stood looking at them from an arched doorway in a ruined wall.

"Clay," Morgan uttered in an uneasy whisper. "The doorway...there's a woman standing in the doorway. She's beckoning us. Oh God!" Memories of the cottage at Stratford and the eerie sounds only she had heard flashed through her mind. Groaning silently, she felt her cold fingers dig into Clay's arm. Suddenly, echoing out of the depths of the ruins, came the sound of a woman's unintelligible, unearthly cry. Again the woman beckoned them. With her heart pounding furiously, Morgan felt a helpless horror creep over her. *This can't be happening to us,* she repeated to herself. Pressing her hands over her eyes, she prayed that when she opened them, the ghastly figure would be gone. After what she felt was an eternity, she opened her eyes and the figure was gone.

"Did you see her, Clay?" Morgan asked imploringly. "Did you see her?"

"Yes, I saw her honey. The muscles in Clay's face were tight and his eyes had taken on a vacant appearance. Putting his arm around her, he drew Morgan close.

"Listen how quiet it's become," Morgan said, looking up sharply.

Except for the gurgling of the Windrush, the area around the ruins had indeed become deathly still. The wind that had been stirring the leaves of the nearby beech trees had suddenly died away as had the sound of gossiping birds.

A thick blanket of bluish grey clouds that had been slowly moving in from the east blotted out the sun and the air felt chill. The ruins that had looked so picturesque in the mottled sunlight, now, in the greying light, presented a lonely and eerie appearance.

"I think we'd better get back to the *Swan*," Clay said as he got up, pulling Morgan to her feet. There was a tone of urgency in his voice.

For a moment, Morgan's eyes lingered on the open archway. *He saw her*, she said to herself. *He saw her. I'm not losing my mind*. "Thank you honey," she said out loud, giving Clay a relieved look. A raindrop fell gently on her upturned face.

A large, cheery fire crackled and popped in the open fireplace, casting a warm glow in the dimly-lit sitting room of the Swan. The rain and wind had arrived with a vengeance, pelting the small, paned windows with a forlorn tattoo. Crashing thunder echoed overhead and flashes of lightning pierced the darkening skies.

The fire and the sherry that Oswald had immediately supplied on their return had dispelled the chill. They had changed for dinner, and Morgan had substituted her dripping mauve crewneck sweater and jeans for a tan, cotton twill skirt, a white turtle-neck top and her newly-purchased moss green pocket cape. Clay, equally soaked, had exchanged his light denim jacket and jeans for a pair of light grey trousers and a wine-colored twill shirt. Seated facing the fireplace in a large ruby-red leather divan, Clay put his arm around Morgan's shoulders and drew her close.

"Honey," he said, giving her an intense smile, "I..."

There was something in Morgan's eyes...a hint of repressed gratitude perhaps, and his smile dissolved into a burst of laughter. It was a wonderful and much-needed release. Morgan, who had been slowly sipping her sherry, could not contain herself either. She gave a snorting little laugh and then doubled up with laughter. She shook so much that she came close to spilling her glass of sherry on her skirt. Her eyes filled and huge tears rolled down her cheeks.

"It must be this inferior grade of sherry," Clay murmured between waves of laughter.

"No, it's not the sherry," Morgan sniffed. "It's that terrible-tasting ale you bought for the picnic. It tasted like burnt carmel." They burst into gales of laughter again.

"May we join you?" The voice was decidedly British and it came from behind them.

"Certainly," Clay said, turning and getting to his feet. "I'm sorry if we disturbed you."

"Not at all. We enjoy a good laugh ourselves, don't we Ellie?"

Around the divan appeared a tall, raw-boned, ruddy-complexioned man, extremely thin and somewhat stooped. His hair, thick and the color of old pewter, gave every indication of being unruly. His eyebrows were dark and bushy. His face was long and clean shaven, his cheeks hollow and his jaw square and firmly-set. His eyes sparkled with a friendly gleam and his brown tweed belted coat, loose-fitting knickers and Argyll socks gave him the look of a typical country gentleman. There was, Morgan thought, an emaciated handsomeness about him.

Ellie, who followed, was equally tall. Her ash-colored hair was swept up, forming a tight knot on the top of her head. A few resistant strands gently brushed her round, full face, punctuated by a short, wide nose that tilted slightly up at the end. She wore a tweed skirt and jacket almost identical in color to her husband's and a white silk blouse knotted at the throat. There was a refined, but neighborly air about her and her hazel eyes seemed to twinkle with friendly amusement as she held out her hand to Morgan, who had risen and was gently wiping her eyes with Clay's hankerchief.

"I'm Ellie—short for Eleanor, and this is my husband, Howard. We're the Beechams."

Howard gently guided his wife to a straight-backed wooden chair that stood closest to the fireplace, took her cane and placed it quietly on the floor next to her.

"I broke my hip this past spring," Ellie said, somewhat hesitantly, "and it's not healing as fast as I'd imagined. I simply could not remove myself from one of those overstuffed chairs that my husband is seated in. I take it you're Americans?"

"Yes we are," Morgan said, regaining her composure and placing her hand on Clay's knee. "We've been in your country a week and love it. It's so beautiful."

"It gets a little somber at times, like tonight," Howard said, crossing his long legs and removing a pipe from his suit pocket.

"He doesn't smoke it," Ellie said, giving Clay and Morgan a reassuring look. "He just likes the feel. I made him give up the habit when I broke my hip."

"What brings you to Swallow Falls?" Howard asked, giving his wife an amused look while elevating the pipe to his mouth.

"We're on our way to Oxford," Clay replied, glancing at Morgan and taking her hand. "We drove down from Stratford and hadn't eaten all day and decided, ... Morgan here decided that this might be a nice place to have a picnic. Morgan is on a sabbatical and will be spending several months at New College. I work for an advertising agency in St. Paul, Minnesota."

"Do you live in Swallow Falls?" Morgan's eyes met Ellie's studying gaze. It seemed that Ellie's lips tightened for just a second.

"It's been a long, long time. Hasn't it, Howard? We were married here the year before the war and have been stationed here ever since, so to speak." There was a wistful tone in her voice as she turned away to watch the fire that had burned away to glowing coals. "Howard was the headmaster of the school in our village for over thirty years and I taught English grammar in nearby Bolton Heath. He spends his time collecting stamps—he is president of the Oxfordshire Philatelic Society—and I tend to my gardening. Our cottage is just up the road and we treat ourselves to mutton dinner here at the *Swan* on Sundays. If you were staying longer we would like you to drop by for a visit."

"Yes, yes, please think about it," Howard said, fingering the bowl of his pipe. "We don't see many Americans here or tourists for that matter. We are sort of insulated, like bees in a hive. I trust you've found a comfortable place for your picnic. As you may have seen, our soil is thin and covered with surface rocks."

"So we noticed," Clay said, getting up and pouring himself a sherry from a large cut-glass decanter that rested near the door. Morgan, anticipating his questioning look, shook her head. "Can I pour either of you a drink? It's sherry."

"No, thank you, Mr. Ashton," Ellie replied brightly, "but do tell us about your picnic."

We found a spot along a footpath near some ruins," Morgan said, taking a sip of her sherry. "We wondered what they were, but we didn't see anyone around to ask." Howard and Ellie exchanged glances.

"That's our main tourist attraction," Howard said, ending his remark with a customary sniff. "What you saw were the remains of an ancient monastery and a manor house that was later built upon the foundation."

"What happened to the manor house?" Clay asked, giving Howard a squinting look. "It looked as if it had been blown up."

"Rightly so, Mr. Ashton," Howard leaned forward and pointed his pipe stem at Clay as if to emphasize his point. "The manor house," Howard continued, "was the home of the Fairfax family for several centuries, but when it was built we don't know. At the time of our civil wars, Bryon Fairfax was master of the house, but unfortunately for the family, he and his brothers sided with the royalists and when King Charles I was defeated by the Parliamentarians in June 1646, their soldiers came and blew up the house."

Morgan gently placed her drink on the polished oak coffee table in front of her, sat back and crossed her long legs. "Were women living at the manor house at the time it was destroyed?" Morgan asked, giving Clay a sidelong glance.

"Why do you ask, dear?" Ellie had reached down and picked up her cane as if preparing to get up. There was something in her voice and the accompanying smile that suggested to both Morgan and Clay that there was more to the story than Howard had so far revealed.

"Well," Morgan said, leaning slightly forward and studying Ellie carefullly. "Clay and I caught sight of a women in a long, grey dress standing in an open archway this afternoon. She beckoned to us. She was there for just an instant. Her appearance was frightening."

The room grew silent except for the muffled sound of voices and the clinking of dinnerware coming from the nearby dining room.

"Mmmm." Howard leaned back and put his pipe back in his jacket pocket. He studied Morgan intently. Ellie's eyes too were riveted on Morgan and her smile had disappeared.

"Our village is small, Mrs. Ashton," Howard said, pressing his freckled finger to his lips, "and we tend to overlook the peculiarities of our neighbors. But there are some who admit to seeing a wraith-like woman about the ruins. No one visits the ruins after dark and our neighbor,Mr. Dingle, swears that on several occasions he has heard a terrible wailing sound coming from the direction of the manor house. Once I took a group of school children to see the ruins. It was a balmy late spring day, but suddenly it got so icy cold that the children complained and we left straightaway. It's alright to be intelligently afraid, Mrs. Ashton."

"The story that has come down to us," Ellie said, sitting bolt upright and placing her hand on her throat "is that a woman playing hide and seek on her wedding night secreted herself in a chest deep within the manor house. Her husband and guests looked for her, but to no avail. The chest lid was self-locking and her cries for help went unaided. We are told that when she was found years later, she was wearing a grey wedding dress. The unearthly wail that is heard from time to time is said to be that of her husband."

The noises from the dining room had subsided and the only sound was the ticking of a large Tambour-style clock that rested comfortably on the fireplace mantle. Morgan's hand trembled slightly as she reached for her drink. Suddenly a bluish flash of lightning, followed by a crackling sound and a thunderous boom, resounded through the room. The lights flickered and then grew dim.

"That was close," Oswald said, emerging from the darkened dining room carrying two tall, wildly-flickering candles. "But I wonder what ails these candles. There doesn't seem to be a draft in here."

"Maybe it's a downdraft from the fireplace," Clay said, somewhat unconvincingly.

"Possibly," Oswald said, giving him a controlled smile, "but I don't believe so. Anyway, dinner is now being served."

Following dinner, Morgan and Clay climbed the narrow, winding stairway that opened to a long, carpeted hall that led to their bedroom.

"Oswald tells me that a figure has been seen walking these halls who disappears through that far wall," Clay said, giving Morgan a sidelong glance while turning the skeleton key in the lock. "People around here think it's a king...possibly Richard III."

Morgan gave him a push into the room. "You are wicked, Clay; wicked, wicked, wicked. I don't want to hear anymore about ghosts. I suppose he said that this room is haunted too," Morgan said, throwing herself on the huge, canopied four-poster bed.

"Yes he did, honey." Clay called from the bathroom. "Every now and again, a guest complains that towels or blankets will come flying out of the linen closet next to the door."

The rain continued to fall in torrents and the sound of thunder and the flashes of lightning seemed to be intensifying. The room was cozy enough, but curiously furnished, Morgan thought, sitting up and surveying her surroundings. No piece of furniture matched; each appeared to have been drawn from a different period. In fact, in the dim light the room presented a compelling contradiction, in a sense, a reflection of what she and Clay had experienced in Stratford and now here.

The sound of water running in the bathroom basin indicated that Clay was attending to his ablutions. Prior to departing into the fearsome night, she and Clay had assured the Beechams that they would join them for breakfast at their cottage in the morning. Much of the dinner conversation had been devoted to their stay in Stratford, and the Beechams, Morgan thought, had been especially interested in her discoveries at the records office.

Morgan had lit two, large pear-shaped candles that rested on platelike holders on the bedside table. Sitting on the edge of the bed, she removed the packet of prints from her purse that they had retrieved that morning. The first two prints, one picturing the Holy Trinity Church with its majestic tower and spire, taken from across the Avon, had turned out beautifully, as had Shakespeare's birthplace. It was the third print that caused Morgan to catch her breath. Her hand trembled as she carefully studied it under the light of the flickering candles. It was the back of the cottage taken on the morning that they had fed the swans. Framed in the patio door was the figure of a woman, dressed in a calico dress and a white apron. She was smiling.

Chapter 5

The Beechams

The rain-swollen cobalt-blue clouds that had earlier enveloped Swallow Falls had given way to a glorious morning, fresh and cool. There was no wind to stir the leaves of nearby trees that hung wet and limp, and except for the chirping of unseen birds, the morning was serenely quiet. A hint of wood smoke hung on the moist air.

"Did Ellie say what their house number is?" Morgan asked, as they emerged from the dim recesses of the hotel into bright sun.

"I believe she said it was seventeen," Clay replied, unlocking their car and rooting in their tote bag in search of their sunglasses.

They had not gone but a few yards before the house numbers indicated they were headed in the wrong direction. Crossing an ancient moss-covered stone bridge that spanned the swollen and rapidly moving Windrush, they made their way past beautifully-preserved thatched and slate-roofed cottages guarded by low stone walls or by waist-high picket fences. Their walls, blanketed by a profusion of yellow and red climbing roses and orange and crimson ivy, the honey-colored cottages presented a warm and inviting look on this glorious fall morning. The chugging of a car laboring up the hill behind them broke the silence, and a moment later, an ancient Mercedes that literally bounced when it came to rest, pulled up beside them.

"Are ye lost?" asked a red, round-faced man who leaned out the window. "Can I render assistance?"

"No, we're not," Clay said, trying hard to be heard over the clanking of the engine. "But thank you anyway."

"Well, cheerio then," and with a wave and a grinding of gears, the man and his car disappeared in a cloud of exhaust smoke.

The thatched stone cottage stood but a few yards from the road and, like the rest, was wrapped in a mixture of red and yellow climbing roses. A dark green plaque embossed with gold letters and set into the wall near the door announced that the cottage belonged to the Beechams.

After several taps of the large, lion-head brass knocker, the door opened and Howard, with a cheery hello and a sweep of his arm, ushered them into a cozy, low-ceilinged room where a fire burned lazily in a fireplace framed in mellowed oak. A vanilla-like fragrance hung in the air and from the back of the cottage, someone was playing *Sentimental Journey* on the piano.

"It's Ellie," Howard said somewhat proudly. "She studied to be a concert pianist, but decided she enjoyed children more than her music. We don't have children of our own."

The music stopped abruptly and Ellie appeared, holding a thick song book in one hand and holding the other out in a greeting.

"I love American song writers," she said, "especially those who wrote songs in the '30s and '40s. Howard and I were hoping you would come; we have been waiting breakfast for you. But please sit down."

"You play beautifully," Morgan said, taking a seat on a faded print couch near the fireplace and motioning Clay to follow her. "Hearing that song makes me think I was born possibly twenty years too late. *I'll Be Seeing You* is one of my favorites, but I don't know when it was written."

"Sammy Fain and Irving Kahal wrote it, I believe, in 1938," Ellie said brightly. "If you would like, I'll play it for you before you leave, or better yet, why don't you play it yourself?"

"How did you know I play the piano?" Morgan asked, looking somewhat suprised.

"She's right seven out of ten times," Howard said, smiling. "It's your fingers. It's the first thing that Ellie notices about a person. Long slender fingers are usually a giveaway."

Breakfast consisted of a steaming cup of tea, scrambled eggs, fried bread, toast, jelly, and sausages, which Ellie referred to as bangers. It was served in a sun-splashed kitchen that looked out on a large, cultivated garden, in the center of which stood a curious vertical stone pillar about four feet high. The stone glistened in the bright morning sun as did the scores of late blooming, water-flecked bushes and flowers.

"Could I offer either of you more eggs, bangers, anything?" Ellie questioned, getting up and pouring Howard another cup of tea. "Could I?" she asked, holding the brown tea pot at eye level.

"Not I," Clay said, holding his stomach.

"Nor I," Morgan repeated. "We often wondered what it would be like to sit down to an English breakfast in a home rather than a restaurant. But I noticed that you didn't serve marmalade."

"Neither of us can stand the spread," Howard said, giving Morgan a look of feigned repulsion. "Now if you two ladies wouldn't mind being alone for awhile, I'd like to take Mr. Ashton over to see our neighbor, Mr. Dingle. I'm sure he has a story or two about the woman that you both saw at the ruins."

"Go right ahead dear," Ellie said, pouring herself a cup of tea. "We'll be just fine."

Out of nowhere, it seemed, a grey and white ball of fur with green eyes, a black nose, pointed ears and a long tail suddenly appeared beside Morgan.

"That's Tabatha," Ellie said with a sigh. "Usually she stays curled up on the rug in front of fireplace in the den when we have company. I see she's taken a liking to you."

"Tell me about that stone in your garden," Morgan said, reaching down and scratching Tabatha behind the ear. "We have seen them in the oddest places. People that we've asked said they had no idea what they represent or who erected them."

"We call her Old Meg," Ellie said, putting her cup down and giving Morgan an amused look. "She has the shape of a woman in a long dress, don't you think? There's another, a rather shapeless stone up on the main highway near the White Hart Pub. But let's repair to the den, these wooden chairs are not for prolonged sitting."

As she began to push her chair back from the table, Morgan felt a sudden and unnerving tingling sensation in her right hand.

"Is something wrong, dear?" Ellie asked, giving Morgan a studied look. "I noticed that you were clenching your hand."

"I have the strangest sensation in my hand," Morgan said, rubbing her hands together and frowning. "It's as if I had touched a low voltage electric wire."

"We don't have a doctor in the village," Ellie said, giving Morgan a concerned look, "but there is one over in Morley Heath."

"No," Morgan said, giving Ellie a faint smile. "The feeling will pass, I'm sure." It was then the memory of a long forgotten event flashed through her mind. It was on that field trip to the Boundary Waters in northern Minnesota a dozen years ago that she had experienced a similar sensation. There were nine students on that trip and she remembered how after they had beached their canoes and were preparing their evening meal, Molly Shaleen, who had a tendency to wander off by herself, came running back to tell the group that she had discovered a strange circle of stones in a field just beyond the woods. The light was failing when they reached the sight, but there, as Molly had breathlessly described, stood a circle of thirty-six rust colored, egg shaped stones. No one spoke for the longest time. Morgan remembered how cool and hushed the area seemed. Not a bird was seen nor heard. As she led the group closer to the circle, Morgan felt the same tingling sensation in her right hand that she was experiencing now. Christopher Stanton and Gretchen Carvell had also complained of a similar sensation in their right hands. "We'd best go back," Morgan remembered saying, as she led the group back to the warmth of their camp fires. That evening as they sat in the flickering firelight, Molly confided that she had stood for a moment inside the circle of stones and felt as if she left her body and was somehow reunited with her parents who were vacationing in France. Her story sent chills up everybody's spine and most of the group, including Morgan, didn't sleep that night. In the morning, she recalled the sensation that she, Christopher, and Gretchen had experienced left them. As they left their campground the next morning, they passed a sheer cliff. High on its face far above the water level, appeared petroglyphs depicting lightning bolts, cross-like symbols, and beetles.

"Are you sure you don't need to see a doctor?" Ellie asked, her face bathed in a cautious smile. "My dear, you left us for a moment."

"I know," Morgan said, smiling apologetically. "The feeling has left, as I knew it would. But thank you for your concern."

Like the kitchen, the den was also bathed in the morning sun. Nestled in the golden oak paneled walls were floor to ceiling bookcases containing hundreds of beautifully bound books, resting quietly in their hand-rubbed bindings. Two well-worn love seats covered in a faded rose-colored print stood on either side of the fireplace in which a low fire gave every indication of going out. Several crimson, glass-shaded reading lamps sitting on highly polished end tables, four wing-backed chairs covered in a plain forest green fabric and a large, somewhat worn Persian rug that all but overlaid the wide plank floor completed the furnishings. The room gave a cozy and lived in appearance. By placing several pieces of kindling on top of the glowing coals, Ellie was able to revive the fire.

"I see that our books have caught your eye," Ellie said, sitting down and wiping her hands on her apron.

"Yes," Morgan said, half turning. "From the age and beauty of the bindings I'd say that you have a fine collection of first editions."

"Yes, that's a hobby of ours. Howard collects Dickens and I collect Hardy. It's expensive and we haven't been able to add to our collection for some time. But you were asking about the stone in our garden."

"Yes," Morgan said, turning and sitting down in the love seat across from Ellie.

"Well, a number of theories have been put forth to explain their origin and meaning," Ellie said, her eyes fixed somewhat absently on the fire. "Stones similar to the one in our garden, some larger, some smaller, are scattered throughout our island. Stonehenge and the circles at Avebury draw the most attention, but there are thousands of others like the ones here at Swallow Falls. Do our stones interest you, Morgan?" Ellie asked, turning and meeting Morgan's steady gaze.

"Very much so." It was the first time that Ellie had used Morgan's first name. "Leonard Crawford, an old and dear friend at Centre College, gave me a book one Christmas entitled, *Secret Stones*. I forget the author's name, but I remember she did a remarkable job of uncovering and describing the legends and folklore that surrounds your standing stones, stone circles, ley lines, and the like." Morgan leaned forward and clasped her hands in front of her.

"We have the book," Ellie said, her voice taking on a matter-of-fact tone. "The author's name is Jane Fields. I haven't read it, but I think Howard has. Tell me what the author said about ley lines. I must confess I know very little about them, but there are people in the village who take their supposed existence very seriously."

Morgan gave Ellie a brief, but surprised look before turning her attention to the fire. It's obvious, she thought, that from the titles of the books that surrounded them, Ellie knows more about ley lines than she admits to. Suddenly, out of nowhere came the uncanny feeling that somehow, somewhere she and Ellie had had this conversation before. Her suprised look caused Ellie to lean forward.

"Are you alright, dear?" she questioned. "Has the tingling sensation returned?"

"No, no," Morgan said, her voice registering a tinge of embarrassment. "I was somewhere else for the moment. But tell me what you have discovered about ley lines in your readings," Morgan said, hurridly, hoping to change the subject.

"Well, we have many researchers and folklorists here in England who firmly believe that rivers of unseen energy run beneath the earth and the stones serve as powerhouses, as well as relay or transmitting stations, for these powerful currents. These rivers, they say, exist all over the world, but the stones are more prevalent in some places than in others. Here in England, the various stone circles, standing stones, hillforts, burial mounds, and other ancient sites are said to align, but for what purpose, no one is quite sure. The Chinese, for example, call these energy lines Dragon Paths."

Except for the crackling of the fire, the room for just a moment, grew very quiet.

"And what does Jane Field say about them?" Ellie continued.

"Basically, the same thing," Morgan replied, shifting her gaze to the fire. "She's especially interested in how birds and animals respond to these rivers or ley lines, and she devotes several chapters relating instances of how they find their way back to their dens or nests from hundreds and even thousands of miles away."

"There was a recent article in our weekly newspaper," Ellie absently remarked, "where birds native to Wales were taken to Boston, banded and released. These same birds were discovered back in Wales two weeks later in the very area from which they were taken. Our discoveries seem to pale when viewed against what remains undiscovered," she concluded, giving Morgan a wan smile.

"Yes," Morgan said, returning Ellie's steady gaze. "One of the fascinating examples Jane Field cites is the Monarch butterfly which flies north out of the Michoa'can Mountains in Mexico in the spring and lays its eggs on leaves of the milkweed plant that grows throughout North America. Once it deposits its eggs the parent dies, but the offspring, guided by some mysterious force, find their way back to the selfsame Mexican mountains that their parents had left earlier. She believes," Morgan said, leaning forward, "that the Monarch, as well as other migrating creatures, are guided to their destinations by standing stones and ley lines. And interestingly, she postulates that we too may be sensitive to the power of the stones and their accompanying ley lines, but for a different purpose. She reasons that for those who are sufficiently sensitive, the stones and lines can act as a guide to new dimensions and realms that we may have experienced in our dreams. She cautions, however, that as we become more and more imprisoned by the ever increasing appeal of technology, our faculty to discern these currents and use them to create a harmony and balance within ourselves is lost."

Ellie, who had been studying Morgan intently, reached for her cane that stood against the fireplace. "Isn't it interesting," she said, giving Morgan an amusing smile. "What we feel passes for persuasive reasoning is often viewed by others as nothing more than musing speculation."

The melodious chimes of the stately Windsor grandfather clock that stood in the living room near the entry sounded ten o'clock.

"It's a comforting sound," Ellie said, standing up. "Can I bring you another cup of tea?"

"Yes, please," Morgan said, standing and following Ellie into the kitchen.

The light, shimmering haze that had earlier enveloped the back yard and garden had evaporated under the warming rays of the sun.

"Are there other standing stones in the village besides the one in your garden and the one near the White Hart?" Morgan asked, holding her steaming tea cup in both hands and gingerly raising it to her lips.

"None," Ellie said, pouring herself a cup of tea and leading the way back into the den. "The two stones are not native to our area and the color and texture makes us believe that it was brought here from Wales. But tell me more about what Jane Field writes about our stones and ley lines. Does she present evidence that ley lines really exist? We *must* have evidence, you know."

"Yes, there is always that illusive matter of evidence," Morgan said, taking a sip of tea. "Jane admits she really doesn't know who placed the stones, when, or for what purpose. She makes the amusing observation that only a dunce requires proof when proof is impossible, but what I found most fascinating about her book was her belief that ley lines and standing stones hold the key to...immortality."

Again, the room for a brief moment grew quiet. Ellie, who had been gazing entrancedly at the fire, turned back toward Morgan and reached for her cup of tea, which rested on a small round table at her elbow. Morgan noticed a strange, faraway look in Ellie's eyes as she sipped her tea. Not knowing if Ellie's religious beliefs regarding immortality were biblically based and, therefore, a subject of some delicacy, Morgan wondered if she had overstepped the bounds of propriety by raising a topic that Ellie might be find disturbing.

"I'm sorry if I've taken us off the subject," Morgan said, giving Ellie an apologetic smile. "Clay tells me I do that quite frequently."

Ellie threw back her head and laughed. "Not at all," she said, reassuringly. "I'm impressed you remember so much about her book. I find as I grow older, my interest in the possibilities surrounding one's immortality becomes more passionate and urgent. What else does Jane Field say on the subject?"

"Well," Morgan said, leaning forward and looking somewhat relieved, "she states that in her research, she came across an extremely rare book that was written early in this century by an anonymous author who maintained that he had deciphered the secret of the stones and their connecting ley lines and thus was able to obtain an everlasting and blissful life without undergoing the unforgiving act of dying. She writes that the book, *Deathless Eternity* is filled with references and descriptions of dreams, and strange and unexplained disappearances of various people throughout England, as well as the rest of the world. Unfortunately, the author didn't reveal how he was able to unlock the stones' secrets. Armed with this book Jane writes that she did some digging in the Doomsday Book and discovered that entire villages in England that were once located along these ley lines have, between censuses, simply disappeared, leaving no trace of their existence. The inhabitants of these villages had also mysteriously vanished. She suggests that ley lines are somehow responsible for these disappearances, but doesn't say how. It may be difficult to think she is convincingly serious, but her writing certainly excites one's curiosity," Morgan said, crossing her legs and shifting her weight slightly. She wondered if she had rambled on too long as she noticed that Ellie's face had remained expressionless and her eyes seemed focused on the crimson shaded lamp that rested on the table to Morgan's left.

As if suddenly aware that Morgan had finished speaking, Ellie uttered a short, mirthless laugh. "It's certainly perplexing," she said, absently poking a glowing log with a fireplace iron. "The line between fact and fancy seems very thin at times. It may be idle gossip, but it has come down to us that a previous owner of our cottage, many, many years ago attempted to dislodge the stone. The townspeople petitioned against its removal, but to no avail. The man, it is said, began to chip away when suddenly his wife and young son expired, his sheep mysteriously died, and he was left penniless. He died in debtor's prison."

"Does it look as if part of the stone has been chipped away?" Morgan asked. Her eyes narrowed as she studied Ellie carefully.

"Oh yes," Ellie replied, smiling faintly. "Large pieces have been cut away from the base that faces away from the kitchen. But there is a story about Old Meg that I haven't mentioned to anyone in the village," Ellie continued, hitching herself forward on the love seat. "It was in the spring of this year. We plant our flower seedlings and seeds early, sometimes as early as January if the weather holds, and on this particular wonderfully warm spring evening, I was out puttering in the garden. It had gotten dark, as I remember, but a bright, full moon so illuminated the countryside that I found I could continue my work without the aid of a lantern. I had been spading near the stone and for just a moment, I placed my hand on it for support. I received such a jolt that I feared I would fall. It was like a bolt of electricity had shot through me. Unfortunately, Howard was away in London at the time, but when he arrived home the next day and touched the stone, he said it simply felt as cold and clammy as it always did. There was a numbness and tingling sensation in my hand and arm for several weeks afterward."

Morgan felt a sudden chill. It was as if a someone had opened a door on a mid-winter night.

"You see, dear," she heard Ellie say as she left the room, "you're not the only person to fall under the spell of the stones."

Voices in the kitchen announced that Clay and Howard had returned, and a moment later Clay appeared, followed by Howard, Mr. Dingle, and Ellie, holding a steaming tea pot above her head.

"I'm pleased to know you," Mr. Dingle said, taking Morgan's hand in both of his. "It isn't often we have Americans in our midst and I understand that your visit was purely accidental. You managed to get lost or something."

Mr. Dingle was a short, balding man with thin lips, a sharp, pointed nose and protruding eyes that looked out through oval spectacles.

"We did manage to get lost, but on purpose," Morgan said, rising to her feet and smiling.

"Mr. Dingle is the local historian, honey," Clay said, taking a cup of tea from Ellie and plopping himself down beside Morgan. "We've been talking about the English Civil War, those mysterious standing stones, hauntings, witches, fairies...we covered a lot in two hours."

"We did lad, we did," Mr. Dingle said, turning toward Howard and nodding. "Our Civil War...ah, that was wretched business, wretched business."

His hand shook noticeably as he took the cup of steaming tea from Howard. "For a nation that prides itself in civility and reason, our land is literally soaked with blood."

"Kenneth here told us of another legend associated with the ruins that I haven't heard before," Howard said, glancing at Ellie, who had seated herself next to Kenneth Dingle and was stirring sugar in her tea.

"Yes, well," Kenneth began by clearing his throat, "it's often difficult to separate folklore from fact, but years ago Mrs. Wallburton, who I always thought was the oldest person living in our village, told me that a sister of Bryon Fairfax, she believed her name to be Charlotte, conceived a child out of wedlock. Fearing that her brother, when he found out, would kill the child by throwing it in the fireplace, as he was told to do with babies who displeased him, she conspired to have the baby secretly smothered and thrown in the Windrush. I have heard the wail of a woman coming from the direction of the ruins on several occasions, usually at night, and the sound literally raises the hair on my head. Needless to say, no one in the village has the courage to go and investigate the source of the wailing."

"Did Clay mention that we saw what we thought was a woman at the ruins yesterday afternoon?" Morgan asked, exchanging a quick glance with Clay.

"Yes he did. It is said, Mrs. Ashton, that the grieving woman, and I believe she grieves terribly for her murdered baby, appears to persons who are about to experience some sort of major change or transformation in their lives."

The room grew silent. The only sounds were the crackling of the fire and the clink of a cup being placed on a saucer.

Morgan half rose from her seat and then sat back down again. She didn't know why. She hadn't felt uncomfortable.

"May I warm your tea, dear?" Ellie asked quietly, noticing Morgan's apparent discomfort.

Without answering, Morgan held out her cup. Her thoughts flashed back to the archway in which the woman in grey had stood beckoning them. Then she remembered something her uncle had said to her many years ago. "Life's events for you, Morgan, will hardly be accidental-tiresome and disfigured at times, but...eminently purposeful.

Faintly conscious that everyone was staring at her, Morgan gave Clay a wistful smile and gently squeezed his hand.

"I say," Howard said, clearing his throat and reaching in his pocket for his pipe, "we don't want to burden the Ashtons with our profane stories. We English are so steeped in myth and fable that it's hard for us to separate fact from idle gossip and untidy thinking."

"Quite so, quite so," Mr Dingle agreed emphatically. "I'm sorry if my words may have disturbed you, Mrs. Ashton, it was not my intention, I assure you. And Howard is right when he says that legends tend to perpetuate themselves, but in the end they often signify nothing."

"Has anyone in the village seen a woman at the ruins and, if so, has the sight changed his or her life?" Morgan asked, turning and giving Clay a quick, but questioning look over the tea cup that she held in both hands. Mr. Dingle,

Howard and Ellie exchanged a brief glance before Mr. Dingle continued.

"Several of our villagers claim to have seen the woman, but if their lives have been changed because of it we don't know."

"There was a girl who lived in the village years ago, so I heard," Ellie said, getting up and putting another log on the fire, "who said that when she and a group of children were picnicking at the ruins she saw a strange-looking woman walking near one of the walls. She didn't tell the rest of the children, but the sight was said to have frightened her badly. It was the girl's grandmother who related the story to me. I believe the girl later went to Oxford and wrote a book. I'll find it before you leave."

"Tell us more about these so-called ley lines that we were discussing earlier, Mr. Dingle," Clay said in an abrupt change of subject.

"Well, Ellie and Howard know as much, if not more about them as I do," Mr. Dingle said, tactfully taking off his glasses and polishing them with an initialed handkerchief.

"Please begin, Kenneth," Ellie interjected.

"Yes, well we know little about the prehistoric peoples that populated our island. Traditions and myths abound, of course, and some of the most fascinating relate to the existence of ley lines, rivers of energy if you will, that are supposed by some to flow beneath the surface of the earth. There are some who staunchly believe these rivers impact us in mysterious ways and are beneficent in certain areas of human conduct." Mr. Dingle paused to reset his glasses. "Ah, that's better. Where was I? Oh yes, these so called ley lines cross and crisscross our entire island, and the standing stones are believed to be energy markers or storehouses, so to speak. Some people report touching them and getting quite a shock."

Ellie and Morgan exchanged brief, but knowing looks.

"There have been many books, and I believe that some are on the shelves here, that tell of the powers embodied in these rivers of energy," Mr. Dingle continued. "We have sworn documents by people who say they have been miraculously healed from some infirmity or illness by touching one of these standing stones. Others say that the stones have brought them good luck, protected their property from storms, cured family members suffering from mental illnesses, and allowed women to produce children when doctors had advised them it wasn't possible. Then, too, there are reports of people living near the great circles who are well over one hundred years old. You can see why it was no accident that castles, and other forts, town halls, churches, cathedrals and various other holy and gathering places were constructed along these ley lines. If your travels take you down to Morning Meadow, you may want to stop in and visit one of our oldest and dearest friends, Mrs. Claire Simmons. She is a noble soul and a most delightful person and one who can tell you much more about these ley lines and standing stones than we can."

Morgan, who had been studying Mr. Dingle intently, suddenly felt a heaviness in her chest and for a moment, it was hard for her to breathe. She reached for Clay's hand.

"Mrs. Simmons is the person..." Clay didn't finish.

"What Clay was about to say," Morgan said, interrupting her husband in mid sentence, "is that Morning Meadow is already in our travel plans and we would be happy to call on Mrs. Simmons when we arrive." Morgan was aware that her face had become flushed.

Mr. Dingle, who had glanced at his pocket watch, suddenly got to his feet looking somewhat startled. "I'm sorry, but I must say goodbye. I have another appointment in the village and I'm already late."

Both Morgan and Clay rose, each taking one of his hands in a parting gesture.

"Yes, yes," he said somewhat hurriedly, "I can't tell you what a pleasure it is to meet both of you. I hope we will meet again someday." He retrieved his cap from a nearby table and then was gone.

The jangling ring of the telephone disturbed the brief moment of silence that had overtaken the room since Mr. Dingle's departure. Excusing themselves, both Howard and Ellie left the room together, leaving Morgan and Clay to exchange a long, perplexed look. Turning away, Morgan stared into the fire that had been reduced to a bed of glowing coals.

"I'm sorry," she said in a half-whisper, "that I barged in like that, but I thought we should keep Mrs. Simmons our secret for awhile longer." She turned back, giving Clay an imposing smile.

At that moment, Ellie reentered the room, cane in hand and limping badly. "English weather is not suited to decaying hips and joints," she said, resting her hand on the arm of the loveseat. "The telephone call is for Howard. He is being called to London for a meeting of stamp collectors and I'll be alone for a day or two. I can't persuade you two to stay over, can I?" she said, giving them a look of anticipated rejection.

"We would like to," Morgan said, getting to her feet and taking Ellie's hand in hers. "You and Howard have been simply marvelous and we can't thank you enough." She gave Ellie's hand a tiny squeeze. "We will always cherish our memory of the Beechams and their hospitality."

"Yes," Clay said, taking Ellie's hand in both of his. "You both have been wonderful. This is not goodbye. Somehow, somewhere, I feel we will meet again."

"Well, then I must find the book that we talked about earlier," Ellie said, her eyes filling with tears. "My...my good mother always said that partings should always be cordial, but not teary. You would think I'm being inconsiderate of her wishes, wouldn't you?"

Morgan and Clay followed Ellie to a book shelf that bordered a large diamond paned window.

"This is the book that I mentioned," she said, reaching up and retreiving a deep blue buckram-bound book. "As I mentioned, it was written by the girl who saw the figure at the ruins many years ago. Her parents and grandparents are long dead and there are no living relatives left in our village."

With Clay standing behind her, his hand on her shoulder, Morgan carefully opened the book to the title page. He felt her stiffen.

"Yes," Ellie said as she studied Morgan intently, "the book is entitled, *Experimenting With Unseen Colors.*"

The muscles in Morgan's face tightened and a mysterious look clouded her eyes as she turned to face Clay. Her finger moved from the title to the name of the authors: Hillary Bowden in collaboration with Matthew Thornton, Oxford University Press, 1974.

"Yes," Ellie said, her face wreathed in a wistful smile, "after she left the village, no one ever heard from her again. It happens sometimes...doesn't it?"

Chapter 6

The Fork in the Road

The passage between Swallow Falls and Oxford was frightfully narrow and serpentine, free of traffic, and as Howard had promised, quietly uneventful. Intriguingly quaint hamlets consisting of a half dozen or so honey-colored and white-washed cottages covered in mantles of ivy or red and pink roses would suddenly appear around a hairpin curve. As she rounded one such curve, Morgan stopped the car to allow a farmer, replete with gaiters, a long stick, and a purposeful walk, direct a meandering herd of black faced and ivory coated sheep across the road into a nearby pasture.

"Can you reach my purse?" Morgan asked, as she braked for a tractor and its waving driver to bounce slowly across the narrow road. "The photos we took at the rear of our cottage are tucked away in there some-place."

Why she had waited until now to present the photos she didn't know, and she wondered how Clay would respond to not having been shown them earlier, especially while they had lain awake at the *Swan* listening to the howling wind and the hammering rain.

"Is there a secret code to the clasp?" Clay laughed, "I never seem to get it opened on the first try."

"Push the button to the side and down," Morgan said, giving Clay a wan smile. Her thoughts were not on the road. She was driving from memory. So many strange and unexplained happenings had occurred since their arrival in England that she questioned her capacity to distinguish what was real and what was illusion. We so looked forward to my sabbatical, she said to herself. Clay, thankfully, would be with her for the entire time and the outcome of her work at Oxford, she felt, held much promise. *But why do I have this chilling feeling that something even more bizarre is going to happen to us? Why? Get ahold of yourself Morgan,* she thought. There has to be an unquestionably sensible explanation for all that has happened. There just has to be.

The sudden appearance of a furry animal scurrying across the road caused Morgan to swerve, sending the contents of the purse tumbling onto the floor.

"Is there something you want to tell me about these pictures before I look?" Clay asked softly as he picked the envelope containing the photos off the floor. Before Morgan could answer, Clay quickly continued. "When I was focusing the camera to get a pictue of you in back of the cottage I saw a woman standing in the patio door," Clay said, his eyes narrowing. "I didn't want to frighten you so I went ahead and took the picture. When I looked again, she wasn't there. Because of the sunlight reflecting on the glass it was difficult to distinguish her features, but she appeared young, maybe in her twenties."

Clay, who had kept his eyes fixed on Morgan while he spoke, noticed that her breathing had increased noticeably.

It took Morgan several seconds to fully comprehend her emotions. "Thank you, honey," she said softly.

"I don't understand," Clay said thoughtfully, half to himself as he turned to face the road. "No one could possibly have been hiding in the cottage, but then again you did hear the front door open. You felt from the very beginning that there was someone unseen in the cottage, didn't you? I wonder if we'll ever discover who the woman is—or if she is?" There was a noticeable sigh in Clay's question.

"I'm sure we will," Morgan said, taking Clay's hand and giving it a squeeze. "And no, I don't believe we have been entirely alone from the time we first set foot in England."

The relief that Morgan felt in knowing that Clay had seen the figure in the patio door registered on her face. It was a moment she would savor.

They had not met a car for the better part of an hour, for which Morgan was thankful. The miles of tall and nearly impenetrable hedges that bordered the road and the sunlight filtering through the overhanging oaks and elms, however, made her slightly dizzy.

Upon slowly navigating another one of the all-too-frequent corkscrew curves there suddenly appeared, as if dropped from the sky, a hay wagon moving at a pace consistent with a brisk walk. Startled, Morgan jammed on the brakes, sending Clay lurching forward. Arms extended, he braced himself against the dash. It was a moment or two before they fully realized that they had avoided a collision.

"You were going so slow anyway honey, that even if you had run up the back of the wagon the driver wouldn't have felt it," Clay said, as he took out his handkerchief and polished his glasses with excessive devotion.

They exchanged looks. It was his way of diffusing a potentially distressing situation. A broad smile creased Morgan's lips and she slumped over the steering wheel, convulsed in sobs of laughter.

"You couldn't have damaged a pane of glass at the speed you were going," Clay continued, his chuckle turning into a giggling laugh. "Let's get out and see how far we have to follow this conveyance," Clay said as he opened the door, scattering a flock of birds that roosted in a nearby hedge.

Morgan, who sat wiping her eyes with her handkerchief, nodded and followed Clay, who had disappeared around the fully-loaded hay wagon.

"Hi there," Clay called to the ruddy-faced, tousled-haired man who wore tattered overhalls and sat atop an ancient red Farmall tractor. The man waved, pushed hard on the brake and brought the machine to a stuttering and squeaking halt.

"Where in the world did you come from?" the man asked as he climbed down and greeted Clay with a firm handshake.

"We've been following you," Clay responded. "We almost nudged you a bit, but Morgan here stopped in time."

"Then you must have a vehicle back there," the man said, peering around the wagon. "We don't see many cars along our road, mostly bicycles and hay tractors like old Jenny here. By the bye, my name is Ralph Thornton and our farm sits on the other side of this hawthorn hedge."

"We're the Ashtons, Clay and Morgan," Morgan said, smiling and holding her hand out in a greeting. "We're on our way to Oxford and some friends in Swallow Falls said that this road would take us there without the benefit of confusing road signs and, of course, traffic."

"Did they now?" Ralph asked, wiping his brow with a tattered handkerchief. "Well, a little further along you'll come to a split in the road. Be sure to take the lane to the right that leads to Oxford, otherwise you're sure to get lost. There are roads around here that you won't find on any map. Some of them get narrower and narrower until they disappear altogether."

The smell of hay tickled their nostrils and both Clay and Morgan sneezed almost at the same time.

"We seem to do things together," Morgan said, handing Clay a tissue and looking at him with amusement.

"Yes, I believe you do," Ralph replied softly, his dark blue

eyes fixed somewhat absently on the hedge that towered behind them. Then, abruptly climbing up and retaking his seat
he said with a broad smile, "I'll be out of your way in a few
minutes. If you come by this way again, stop for a spot of
tea. You'll find the land in these parts peaceful and filled
with wonders beyond these hedges." Trailing puffs of white
smoke, the tractor lurched forward and slowly disappeared
around a tree shaded curve.

"I'm hungry," Clay said as they made their way back to
the car. "What do you think is in that colorful tin basket that
Oswald carried to the car this morning?"

"Probably beef sandwiches, lemonade and tapioca pud-
ding," Morgan replied. "The English seem fond of beef
dishes and puddings."

"Well, I hope it's not mutton," Clay said, opening the
passenger door and rummaging for the basket.

The miles of hedgerows that had lain so chokingly close
to the road had slowly disappeared, replaced by long
stretches of low, moss-covered, stone walls. The relief on
Morgan's face was apparent as she glanced at Clay, who was
busy examining the contents of Oswald's food basket.

Before them lay a long, picturesque valley bordered by
gently-slopping, tree-covered hills. The slanting, morning
sun screened by huge billowy clouds, cast dark, moving
shadows across the hillsides and over the undulating valley
floor. Nestled among the folds of the hedge-bordered fields,
dressed in various shades of green and gold, were cozy looking farmhouses. In the far distance, a ruler straight canal lazily ferried several boats to some unknown destination. To
the left and far down the valley Morgan saw the faint outline
of a steepled church and a tree-shaded village situated
alongside a shimmering, meandering river. The sudden and
welcome appearance of a shaded turnout offered both a re-

spite from the taxing drive and afforded an opportunity to indulge their appetites.

"Let's stop here and enjoy the view," Morgan said, turning to see what Clay had discovered in the basket.

Clay was intently examining several thick roast beef sandwiches wrapped with wax paper, and for a moment, neither was aware of a man resting his arms on the top of an ancient wooden gate that stood but a few yards away from the driver's side of the car.

"I'm sorry," Morgan said, quickly rolling down the window. "We couldn't resist the view. I hope our stopping hasn't disturbed you."

"Not at all," the man replied, touching the brim of his flat cap and smiling. "The view is a beautiful one, especially on such a sun-filled morning."

Clay, who had returned the sandwiches to the basket, leaned over Morgan and gave the man a half wave.

"Yes," the man continued," the valley is subject to sporadic showers and on many days the mist and rain obscure the Dorchester Canal down there. However, today it gives the appearance of a shining ribbon, don't you think?"

"Do you get much rain?" Morgan asked, somewhat absently, taking a cup of hot coffee from Clay's outstretched hand.

"Tis an interesting valley to be sure," the man responded, as if he had not heard the question. His gaze seemed thoughtfully fixed on some scene in the distance. "That village and the surrounding countryside way off there gets very little rain. The sun shines bright on many days when the rest of the valley is dripping."

"A freak of nature, no doubt," Morgan said, not loud enough for the man to hear.

At that moment, Morgan was struck with the uneasy feeling that she had heard the man's exact words before. As she turned toward him, his face, for the briefest of moments, seemed vaguely familiar.

The sudden change in Morgan's features did not go unnoticed.

"Are you alright, honey?" Clay asked, reaching for her hand.

The feeling that had so abruptly appeared, dissolved just as suddenly.

"Yes," Morgan said, giving Clay a quizzical smile. "I'm fine. I was somewhere else for just a moment."

"We're on our way to Oxford," Clay called out the window, stretching across Morgan. "We were told to keep to the right at a fork in the road, but he didn't tell us how far it was. "You seem tense, honey," Clay whispered. Did you feel something?"

"I'm fine, honey, really I'm fine." Morgan's smile was reassuring.

"Yes," the man said, making an indifferent gesture, "you were given the right directions. You'll come to a split in the road about a mile from here. Be sure to keep to the right now. People have been known to get frightfully lost by going to the left."

"Those were Ralph's words," Morgan said thoughtfully.

"Ask him if he knows where the other road leads," Clay said, pouring himself a cup of coffee.

"Do you know..." Morgan began, slowly turning her head. The question would go unasked, as the man had suddenly disappeared.

Aware that Clay was watching her intently, Morgan felt her cheeks warm with a rush of color. She laughed a soft, uncertain laugh. *I must understand, I must understand, she repeated to herself, that somehow we have lost control. Yes that's it, we have lost control. But of what?*

"What are you thinking?" Clay asked pensively, as his gaze drifted back toward the gate.

A bird fluttering in one of the immense elms had caught Morgan's attention and Clay noticed a faraway look in her eyes.

"How could someone disappear so quickly?' she asked under her breath. After a long pause, her eyes also riveted on the gate. "And isn't it strange that we didn't meet a car coming or going on this stretch of the road? The only signs of life were Ralph and the man at the gate. It all seems so unreal."

The sun filtering through the leaves created a dappled look on the surrounding grass and on the weathered wayside table upon which Clay had spread the contents of the picnic basket. A soft warm breeze gently stirred the leaves that were tinged in colors of gold and red.

Brushing aside a family of visiting bees, Clay rewrapped the remains of their picnic lunch and joined Morgan, who was quietly watching a flock of swallows and sparrows swoop and glide over a nearby meadow carpeted in patches of purple, red, and yellow wild flowers.

"Besides the disappearance of the man at the gate, what else startled you?" Clay asked, breaking the silence and giving Morgan a long and deliberate look. He was well aware of the depth of Morgan's feelings and her thoughtful, appraising expression aroused his suspicion that there was more on her mind than the odd disappearance of the man at the gate. "Did something frighten you?" he asked again.

There was a long pause. Morgan's elbows were resting on the table and her hands were clasped under her chin. Their eyes met.

"No, not frightened, but for just a moment I felt that I had heard the man's words spoken before. At the same time, his face seemed vaguely familiar. The vision, or whatever it was, happened so fast that now I'm not sure what I heard or saw."

"What words, honey?" Clay asked, his eyes narrowing.

"It was his comment about that village far down the valley being sunny when the rest of the countryside was dripping," came Morgan's pensive reply. "For as long as I can remember," Morgan continued, "I've had this recurring dream about a village situated in a beautiful valley with trees and colorful wildflowers all around. The air is always perfumed with the smell of lilacs and I've seen people boating on a river that meanders through the village. Each time I've had this dream there is more to see and so that I wouldn't forget, I've been jotting down what I remember about this particular dream each morning. What I saw in that valley, the village, the river, everything was identical to what I've seen in my dream."

Morgan stopped. Her eyes searched Clay's face, which remained expressionless. She must make sense out of her fragmented thoughts. *What is he thinking?* she asked herself anxiously, *and what is happening to me?* No, she told herself, she wasn't frightened. Just the opposite. Did she have words to describe to Clay the overwhelming feeling of peace and total contentment that she felt while looking down that broad, beautiful, and serene valley?

For a moment, the only sound was the soft rustling of the leaves and the chirping of several sparrows who were perched in a nearby elm tree.

Sensing the struggle that Morgan was feeling, Clay stretched out his arms and took her hand in both of his. There was a long pause as they searched each other's faces.

"Honey," Clay began nervously. He took a deep breath and shifted his gaze to the meadow beyond. "I didn't see the village that you and the man at the gate saw. I can't say it wasn't there; I just didn't see it. I saw the canal, and the canal boats, but I didn't see the church steeple or the trees or the village."

Morgan felt her cheeks grow warm. She remembered that Clay had not responded when she called his attention to the village, nor did he when the man referred to its weather. She also sensed the struggle that Clay was experiencing. He had chosen his words carefully and had said them slowly so as to not be misunderstood. Morgan calmly met his steady gaze.

"Tell me what you saw," she said softly, leaning forward and placing her folded hands in her lap.

"I don't know now what I saw, honey," Clay replied, uneasily. Turning, he poured the last of the coffee into their paper cups. "I thought I did, but now I'm not sure. I've never been very good at reconciling the inexplicable, have I?" A faint smile creased his lips.

"Then again, I may have for a moment revisited my dream," Morgan said, giving Clay a kindly smile. The feeling of total peace and serenity that had permeated every fiber of her being remained strong. It was an experience to savor. I won't injure it by excessive analysis, she told herself.

"But the man at the gate also referred to the village," was Clay's thoughtful response.

"Maybe he didn't exist either," Morgan said, pulling Clay to his feet. "We'd better be on our way if we plan to find our cottage before nightfall."

The spires, towers, and domes of Oxford lay before them in a lush green basin surrounded by low semiwooded hills. Clay, who had taken the wheel had, at Morgan's urging, stopped at a turnout on the brow of a hill, giving them a panoramic view of the city.

"I can't believe we're here," Morgan said, stepping out and walking around to the driver's side of the car.

A soft breeze tinged with the smell of wood smoke ruffled her hair. The red tile and blue slate roofs of the

tightly-packed houses and the groupings of college buildings cast in the color of honey gold by the waning sun gave
the city and the surrounding countryside a warm and inviting look. Clay, who had also deserted the car, stood behind
Morgan and wrapped his arms around her waist.

"I wonder which of the two rivers our cottage is on?"
Clay said in a half-whisper as he gave Morgan a little
squeeze.

"Theopholis said it was on a branch of the Cherwell,"
Morgan replied, folding her hands over Clay's. They stood
for several moments alone with their thoughts.

Morgan remembered how insistent Leonard Crawford
had been about choosing Oxford for her advanced studies in
Speculative Religions.

"Can the mind understand itself?" he once asked her.
"The road leading toward an answer may very well pass
through Oxford," he had told her.

During the year before his retirement, Leonard had often disappeared for days, leaving his teaching duties to his
assistants. When he returned he would call her, saying that
there was something important he wanted to discuss. She
remembered how wistful and pensive he was after returning from one of his mysterious sojurns. The question was
typical of his approach to subjects with elusive meanings,
but his comment about Oxford had suprised her. During
her undergraduate days at Severn she had exchanged letters with a Bertie Frankland who, at the time, was studying
economics at Oxford's Merton College. She remembered
how he had sent her his college's red and black striped tie
which she wore along with jeans and a white shirt on
spring frolic days on campus. On occasion, Leonard would
wear the very same tie, but he never mentioned Merton
and she never questioned him about it. At one of these re-
flective meetings, Leonard had commented how he felt we

had become willing prisoners to our useless truths and traditions.

"There are worlds," she remembered hearing him say, "that our minds and our senses have not penetrated. With billions of cells in our brains, we may someday find that our heaven lies somewhere within the mysterious realm of the brain. To meet one's personal heaven, my dear Morgan," he had once said, "one must be willing to give up such dearly held values as hate, greed, destructive rage, selfishness and the drive to succeed at all costs."

Morgan found herself smiling as she recalled how his opinions had provoked stinging responses from his colleagues and how they had accused him of indulging in inventive hypotheses to comfort his own conscience. The sound of a train whistle broke the silence.

"We'd better be on our way," Clay said, giving Morgan a peck on the cheek. "The sun's almost down."

"I love Theopholis' directions," Morgan said, carefully examining a hand-written sheet with the aid of a penlight. "Take a right at the Camel's Eye Pub, watch for the cottage with the blue door and the large lion's head knocker. You'll see the tower of St. Mary's Church. Turn left at the church and follow the narrow lane which abuts the cemetery. You'll pass Ye Old Tea Shop which serves the best Shepherd Pie and clotted cream in the shire."

The sun had set, leaving a brilliant blush pink and orange glow in the cloudless sky as they arrived at the corner of Bunting Street and Stillwater Lane.

"Turn left on Stillwater," Morgan said, her voice rising with excitement. "Oak cottage should be at the end of the lane."

And so it was. At lane's end stood a small, white-washed thatched cottage with a maroon door and latticed, eyebrowed windows. A cool rose-scented breeze stirred the slender stalks of pampass grass that flanked the narrow brick walkway which meandered through a large and well-manicured red and yellow rose garden on its way to the door.

"It's wonderful," Morgan said, holding the door open for Clay who was struggling past her with the last of their luggage.

"I wonder if the refrigerator is well stocked," Clay replied somewhat breathlessly, giving Morgan an amused look. "I'm famished and I don't think we could find our way out of here in the dark to find a restaurant or a grocer's."

"How can you be hungry at a time like this? There's so much to see." Morgan's voice trailed off as she disappeared into the living room. "Come look, honey. Our cottage has a brick fireplace and a piano. And there's a wooden porch swing in the back yard. And look, the river runs right past our back door and oh, what a beautiful flower garden. Clay, let's go out and sit on the swing for awhile. We had a porch swing in Fincastle and I remember how I enjoyed it."

They had been relaxing on the swing, Morgan with her ankles crossed in front of her and Clay giving the swing a gentle push every so often. The only sound was the gurgling of the river and the cry of several nightbirds hidden in the branches of a nearby tree.

"Honey," Clay whispered, placing his arm around Morgan's shoulders, "have I told you how much I love you?" He took her hand and kissed it.

"I'll never tire of hearing it," Morgan replied softly, resting her head on Clay's shoulder. "I...." She didn't finish.

From somewhere near, the melodic sound of a harp and a woman singing could be heard drifting on the mild evening air. Clay felt Morgan stiffen. Clay straightened, too and stopped the swing. A sudden brisk breeze rattled the leaves on an overhanging tree.

"What is it, honey?" Clay asked in a quiet, but deliberate tone, his eyes fixed on a shadow that he thought had moved quickly across the garden.

"It's that song," Morgan said closing her eyes. "My mother sang *Greensleeves* to me when I was little before she tucked me in bed and Clay...I think it's coming from within our cottage."

Chapter 7

The Meeting

It was Monday morning and after a hurried breakfast at the cottage and a brisk walk through mist-shrouded streets, Morgan and Clay stood before a massive oak door upon which appeared a large, brightly polished brass plaque with the name Theopholis S. Weeks engraved on it. Looking bedraggled and shaking droplets of water off their raincoats, they both took several deep breaths and exchanged glances that hinted at both wonder and amusement. Morgan nodded as Clay gently knocked on the door.

"Come in, come in, the door is open, just depress the handle and hang your raincoats on the tree," the voice with a distinct Scottish accent called.

Seated in an ancient high-back wooden wheel chair at the end of a library table behind mountains of papers in studied disarray was a short, heavy-set man with a florid face, a high forehead, a bulbous nose, and a full wide mouth set firmly in a double chin. His large head was devoid of hair, except for a few whispy white strands that hung limp down the back of his neck and over his ears. There were large bags under his piercing, gray-green eyes. As he peered at them over the top of narrow rectangular wire rimmed spectacles, he looked for all the world, Morgan thought, like Benjamin Franklin.

"Beastly day," the man in the wheelchair said reprovingly as he wheeled himself around the table, his large hand outstretched in greeting. "I'm Theo Weeks and I take it you're the Ashtons."

"We are indeed the very wet Ashtons," Clay said, helping Morgan off with her raincoat.

"I can't believe we're really here," Morgan said, smiling and taking Theo's hand, "and we can't thank you enough for your attentive courtesies. Both Clay and I..."

"Come, come, there is no need for that. Some of my colleagues delight in accoladeous remarks, but I often find them undeserved and quite forgettable. But, come warm yourselves by the fire and tell me about your adventures while I pour you a cup of tea. You both drink tea, I presume?"

"I'd much prefer brandy on a day such as this," Clay said, giving Morgan a wink and taking a chair next to her by the fire.

"Ah...now there's a man who understands one's capacity for real hospitality," Theo said, handing each a cup, permanantly anchored to a saucer. "But custom requires a certain allegiance and, according to tradition, our rooms must remain unravaged by strong drink. But," Theo paused. Reaching into a dark blue cloth bag that hung from a hook on his wheelchair, he produced a silver flask. "There are times when stuffy tradition must be softened by a bit of aeration, do you agree?"

The burning logs in the small fireplace cast a warm glow on the walls of the rectangular room adorned with bookcases, ancient looking maps, and paintings of cottages nestled in flowery landscapes. At one end of the room stood a half dozen threadbare, wing-backed chairs situated so that they formed a semi-circle. At the other, three low-backed leather chairs with rounded arms surrounded the fireplace. Two dimly lit brass floor lamps with old fashioned fringed shades gave the room a cozy and inviting appearance.

"If I remember your letter correctly, Morgan, you and

Clay have been in England for over a week before arriving here," Theo began offhandedly, taking a sip of brandy and eyeing them over the lip of the cup. "I'm interested in your impressions, our soggy landscapes notwithstanding."

"Driving in this morning and seeing the towers, the steeples and the surrounding hills shrouded in a fine mist is a sight we'll long remember," Morgan replied, returning Theo's steady gaze. "We did, as I mentioned in my letter, spend several days in Stratford in a rented cottage. A distant relative of mine had emigrated to the the Virginia Colony in the early part of the 18th century and on our last day in Stratford I spent several hours at the public records office combing through old records while Clay did some shopping."

"I trust you both found your pursuits rewarding and your stay at the cottage a pleasant one?" Theo asked, leaning over and giving the flame-blanketed logs a thrust with a pick-like poker.

"There were several occurrences at the cottage at Stratford that we couldn't explain," Clay said, giving Morgan a sidelong look. "Then again, last night while we were relaxing in the backyard of our cottage here in Oxford, we heard a woman singing and it sounded as if it was coming from inside the cottage. But we don't want to bore you with experiences that we can't explain."

"Not at all, not at all, please continue," Theo said, his voice rising. "The inexplicable always fascinates."

"Ever since we landed in England Clay and I have experienced a generous amount of unaccountable happenings," Morgan said, giving Theo a wan smile. "For example, we thought we were alone in the cottage at Stratford, until we looked at a picture that we had taken on our last day there. Then there were sounds, voices really that I heard, but Clay didn't. They frightened me and..."

"What kind of sounds?" Theo interrupted, moving his wheelchair forward ever so slightly.

"Clay had gone out to find a grocery store and I may have been dozing by the fire, but I thought I heard someone call the name of Duncan Alister. It startled me. The voice was loud. I had no idea where it came from. Then on our last night at the cottage, I heard the name called again. Clay and I were standing in the kitchen. He didn't hear it, but the voice was loud and distinct. The voice seemed to come from everywhere yet...nowhere."

For a moment the room grew silent, broken only by the faint hissing of the burning logs.

"You mentioned a picture," Theo said, clearing his throat and adjusting the plaid blanket that covered his legs.

"Yes I have it," Clay said, retrieving it from his corduroy jacket pocket and handing it to Theo. Again the room grew quiet.

"Can you turn on another light and bring me that magnifying glass on the desk, Clay?' Theo asked, bowing his head for a closer look at the photograph. "Do either of you recognize the woman?"

"No. She's young and she seems to be wearing a dress commonly worn in the last century, doesn't she?" Morgan said, leaning forward and resting her arms on her knees.

"Yes...time, how do we define it, how do we explain it?" Theo asked, looking up and resting his chin on his clasped hands.

Aware that his remark had left Morgan and Clay looking puzzled, he hurried to apologize.

"I'm sorry, the picture is indeed interesting, but the point of my question may be basic to understanding how a woman could appear in a window of your unoccupied cottage. My father spent his last days seeing the world through an invalid's window and my fate may well parallel his so the meaning of time is not a matter of indifference to me."

"And to me," Morgan replied, leaning forward and clasping her hands.

"My doctoral dissertation dealt in part with our obsession with time, which provides, I suppose, a convenient ruler against which we measure our lives, but in reality is nothing more than an accepted abstraction."

Theo had touched on a subject that struck a familiar chord and Morgan felt her cheeks grow red with excitement. She glanced at Clay, who was examining the contents of his cup with a bemused look.

For a moment, the room became suddenly quiet as a gust of wind sent a shower of glowing coals onto the brick hearth. The only sound was the rain drumming against the four diamond paned windows that overlooked the old city wall.

"A melancholy day to be sure," Theo said, pouring himself another drink and handing the flask to Clay. "An abstraction you say. Well, now that's an interesting consideration. And what else does your dissertation reveal about the essence of time?"

"One of the questions that my thesis raised," Morgan replied, choosing her words slowly and carefully, "was whether today, tomorrow and yesterday exist simultaneously. As we know, not everything becomes obvious through explanation and thankfully, my thesis review members were all talented in the art of unobtrusive cross-examination."

"And what conclusions did you arrive at in your theoretical effort to leap the time barrier?" Theo asked somewhat absently, while leaning over and placing another log on the fire. "It's interesting," he continued, "that your review panel was so sympathetic. My experience with colleagues on such panels often bordered on unbridled derogation."

"I thought derogation was the sole property of advertising agencies," Clay remarked, giving Theo a look of feigned surprise.

"We tend to comfort ourselves with the notion that our impressions are unique, but in this case I can assure you, yours is totally inaccurate." Theo's somewhat slow response was couched in a sly grin. "But what of your conclusions?" he persisted, taking a renewed interest in the cup he was holding.

"Isn't it interesting," Morgan responded in a low, soft voice, "that in a dream that may last a half hour or so, our unconscious minds seem quite able to override the so called time barrier. In doing my thesis, I interviewed several hundred people from all walks of life who remembered having dreams in which they were reliving an event from the distant past when suddenly the dream changed and they were witnessing or participating in an event in the present. Others related how in their dreams they found themselves experiencing scenes in the present, but suddenly found themselves witnessing an event that they said did indeed occur sometime later. A dream that spans many years can begin and end in a matter of minutes."

"And what say you, Clay?" Theo asked after a thoughtful pause. "Do Morgan's ruminations strike a familiar chord?"

"It's interesting," Clay responded, his gaze fixed on the fire. "I don't know if this recurring dream I have is set in the past, present, or future. I do know that my dream takes me to a place, a wonderfully familiar place, of narrow, unpaved country roads, of tree-shaded farms nestled in folds of hills. I see fields of corn and all manner of growing things, including beautiful scented flowers. I never see a car though, but I see shops and people. Everything seems serene and peaceful."

"Is it a place that you would like to escape to?" Theo asked, reaching in his bag and producing a pen and a notebook.

"Very much so," Clay sighed, giving Theo a controlled smile.

There was a pause while Theo scribbled a name and an address on a piece of paper and handed it to Morgan.

"People wanting to escape into their dreams," Theo said, giving Morgan a challenging look, "and then having those dreams later become a reality may be just a comforting illusion, but on the other hand....."

"On the other hand," Morgan interrupted, "what my paper attempted to show was that one's personal attachment to a place or a person, in a dream state, if strongly desired and revisited in subsequent dreams, just may attune our senses to a totally new reality. I think Leonard summed it up best when he said our minds, or souls if you like, house an unending stream of possibilities seeking to be expressed."

"And I agree," Theo said, leaning over and giving the burning logs another poke with the iron. "I believe that this so called phantom reality co-exists alongside ours, but how to enter it, that's the conundrum. The author that appears on the piece of paper I gave you believes that to enter this wonderful trouble free reality requires a sacrifice. More specifically, he postulates that one must be able to purify or abandon long-held values, desires and beliefs such as greed, aggression, hatred, and other self destructive behaviors that combine to imprison the mind or soul if you will. Much sober thought and reflection are a necessary beginning, but my personal belief is that for many, the idea of changing their beliefs, as well as their actions, will continue to remain a nauseating prospect, regardless of the rewards that may lay beyond."

Leonard, Morgan remembered, had on occasion, expressed those very same thoughts about how the abandonment of destructive behaviors and beliefs opens and enlarges our senses to new meanings. Staring glassidly at the fire, she recalled how a number of their colleagues at Centre had criticized his hypothesis that dreams are but doors to a new reality. "His assumptions were tantamount to reflection without personal observation," they said, "and as such, they were nothing more than polished nonsense."

Suddenly aware that all eyes were focused on her, Morgan reached for Clay's hand. "Sorry," she said, her voice tinged with embarrassment. "I was somewhere else for a moment."

"Yes, she does that from time to time," Clay said, squeezing Morgan's hand and giving Theo an amusing smile.

"Yes, yes," Theo said, nodding vigorously. "We all have a penchant for doing that from time to time. But let's agree for the moment that our dream states ignore with impunity our perceptions of time and space. Let's also agree that philosophic detachment must prevail in certain instances. Doubt may or may not produce wisdom, but knowledge, as well as intuition, also carry their own train of limitations."

The silence that had greeted Theo's last remarks was broken by the ringing of a small bell that hung from a cord just inside the door.

"It's my personal summons," Theo said, with an impish grin. "Only a few of my friends know of the existence of its trigger; it's so well camouflaged in the door's scroll work. Come in, come in, the door's unlocked."

Standing in the doorway, his fawn-colored raincoat shedding droplets of water on the highly polished floor, stood Leonard Crawford, his rain-washed sandy hair matted to his head.

"I forgot my umbrella," he said with an embarrassed smile.

Removing his soggy raincoat and hanging it on a hook attached to the door, he quickly strode over and grasped Clay's hand. Morgan, looking somewhat startled at the sudden appearance of her friend, rose slowly, as if still uncertain about the visitor's identity.

"Theo and I cooked up this little surprise meeting," Leonard said, edging past Theo and taking Morgan's hands in both of his. "I know we had planned to meet next week, but I had a trunk call from Cheerio, your faithful travel representative, this morning and she wondered how you and Clay had survived your cottage stay in Stratford. Survive, by the way, was her word-not mine."

"Cherrio seems to possess extrasensory powers," Clay said, clearing his throat.

"'Survive' is a bit melodramatic," Morgan responded in a barely audible voice. "Endured is a much more descriptive and accurate term."

"Tea or brandy, friend?" Theo asked, wheeling himself backward to retrieve a steaming tea pot that had been resting on an aged-looking hot plate.

"Tea with a lump of sugar, please. It's so nice to see both of you again," Leonard said, his face bathed in a wide smile as he stirred the lump of sugar into his cup.

"And you," Morgan said, hitching herself foreward with her hands clasped tightly in her lap.

Leonard's sudden apearance was not suprising. No, Morgan said to herself, she was accustomed to him dropping by unexpectantly. But she wondered if the word 'survive' was Cheerio's or his. And why had she called Leonard? Cheerio knew their itinerary and the phone numbers where they could be reached. Strange, she thought.

"We were discussing the tangled web of time, dreams and reality, subjects that consumed many an evening back at Centre," Morgan said brightly, hoping that Leonard had not detected the consternation that she felt.

"Ah, yes," Leonard responded, sipping his tea gingerly. "Has Theo shared his dictums on these subjects?"

"Unfortunately not," Clay said, giving Leonard a look of mock displeasure. "He's been playing the devil's advocate, but we suspect..."

"Quite so," Leonard interrupted. "Theo has written extensively on what he calls the unfamiliar dimensions of time and space, and it is he who has vulcanized my own interest and enthusiasm for the subjects. You know, of course, that his book, *The Dubious Present*, is a classic critique of our accepted principles relating to time and..."

"Come, come Leonard let's not bore our guests with uninvited, adulatory sermons," Theo said, giving Leonard a frowning glance over the tops of his glasses, which had slipped halfway down his nose. "I relish the opportunity to listen, rare as that opportunity is, to the solemn pronouncements of my esteemed colleagues on subjects upon which there has been a profusion of incoherent thought. So, my dear friends, share with me your thoughts and if you like, your dreams."

There was a moment of silence as Theo passed his flask around. Clay, taking his cue from Morgan, placed another log on the fire.

"And what, specifically, have you been discussing on such a melancholy day?" Leonard asked, placing his cup down on a nearby table and resting his chin on his clasped hands.

"We were talking about the shadowy world of dreams and how our consciousness of them does not seem to be governed by any principle that we have yet discovered," Morgan said, turning toward Leonard and curling her legs under her.

"A teasing subject not given to idle conversation," Leonard said, stirring another lump of sugar in his brimming cup. Caught in the blue orange glow of the fire, Morgan noticed that Leonard's eyes had taken on a far and away look.

"In a sense," he continued, "we are prisoners of our senses and the prescribed doctrines that emanate from them. We live in a primitive environment in which our senses and our images are daily conditioned by the prevailing notions of time and space, but let's suppose for a moment that the mind is capable of freeing itself from this self-imposed incarceration."

"The question of 'how' came up awhile ago," Clay interjected, giving Morgan a questioning look, "but I don't remember that we arrived at an answer. Morgan and I have discussed at length the question of what's real and what's imagined. In the world of advertising, *imagery is what's real,* not *what's real is imagery,* if you know what I mean."

The room grew quiet for a moment.

"You have a point, Clay," Leonard said, glancing away from the fire and studying Clay with a renewed interest. "But even if we grant that advertising is capable of seducing reality by cleverly-constructed images, the entire process is still a prisoner of time. Let me illustrate. Several years ago, a friend said she had recently travelled to northern Minnesota with a friend to spend several days at a resort on Lake Vermilion. On their way, they stopped at a petrol station in a town where another friend, an older man, had grown up. As she was paying for her bill, she said she turned and came face to face with a young man whose features precisely matched a photograph of her older friend who had been taken taken years before. She was so startled by the resemblance that she admitted staring at the man for a long moment. She said he returned her studied gaze, but made no attempt to enter into a conversation. She then said she went outside for the express purpose of waiting for him, but he didn't appear. She confided in her traveling companion what she had experienced. After what felt like an eternity, she reentered the station, described the man who had stood behind her and asked the attendant what had happened to him. The attendant said he remembered her, but did not see anyone behind her. In addition, there were no other cars at the pumps. Needless to say, she departed the station both mystified and somewhat embarrassed. Had she actually seen her older friend as a young man? Had she, for a moment, stepped back in time, a retro-cognition, if you will? She swears she saw her friend as a young man. If she did, how then does this alter our perception of time and space?"

The room grew silent again. Morgan's gaze was drawn to the fire and the wispy fingers of smoke that lazily drifted up the chimney. Clay too seemed deep in thought as he stared absently at the contents of his nearly empty cup. Theo, with a renewed interest and with the aid of his magnifying glass, studied the photograph of the woman standing in the patio door that Morgan had given him. Leonard, quite unnoticed, had gotten up and had retrieved a piece of paper from his raincoat pocket.

"Did your friend say that she had been thinking about her older friend just before her encounter?" Morgan asked softly.

"Yes she had," Leonard replied, looking up from the piece of paper he was holding. "The petrol station, she said, was one of those relics of bygone days. She of course related her experience to her friend who said he had been a customer there many times during his younger days."

"I would have guessed he was not on her mind just then," Morgan said, looking somewhat surprised.

"I'm not sure it would have made any difference whether she had or hadn't," Leonard replied with a shrug of his shoulders. "What she said she saw was not an apparition, but a person of substance. Now it can be argued, and I feel rightfully so, that of our five senses, sight may be the most limiting. There are two of our colleagues here at Oxford, both forensic anthropologists who postulate that the sight sensors of our primitive ancestors were equipped to only see various shades of grey, but in the intervening millenia, our sight sensors have progressed to where we are aware of many more colors in the light spectrum. My personal belief is that our brain, which orchestrates and connects incoming sight patterns, is capable of perceiving many additional colors, patterns and sights, including those of a higher vibrational value. The trigger in my friend's case seems to have been a thought...a thought relative to her older friend. Somehow her thought had penetrated the wall of time and brought into the present a figure, her friend from the past. Thoughts, however, may not be the only triggger, but there is a growing body of evidence that they play an important role."

"Is your hypothesis broad enough to explain the figure in this picture?" Theo asked, leaning over and handing Leonard the snapshot of the cottage.

"There's a figure of a young woman in the patio door," Leonard responded, giving Theo a puzzled look. "I don't understand."

"It's the cottage we rented in Stratford before arriving here," Morgan said in a voice hardly above a whisper. "Our bags were packed and we were ready to leave when we took the picture. There had been no one in the cottage."

Leonard and Theo exchanged quick glances.

"Do either of you recognize her from an early snapshot perhaps, or someone that you may have met albeit briefly?" Leonard asked, somewhat cautiously.

Both Morgan and Clay shook their heads. There was a pause as Leonard continued to study the photo with the aid of Theo's magnifying glass. Looking up, he handed the photo to Clay, who noticed that Leonard's hand trembled a bit. Morgan noticed it, too.

"Our eyes can at times be very deceptive," Leonard said, resting his elbows on the arms of his chair and forming a triangle with his thumbs and forefingers. "As with the experience of my friend, the camera in this instance may have succeeded in breeching the time barrier, capturing a figure who may have lived or owned the cottage years ago. Another explanation may be that the figure is a thought form projected by a woman who is currently alive, but is now much older. One can imagine a number of other expositions, but it's possible that the mystery may, just may, resolve itself before you return to Centre."

The sudden tinkling of the door bell broke the quiet that had settled over the room.

"It's not one of my students," Theo said, looking somewhat annoyed as he wheeled himself toward the door.

The sound of the door opening was met with a moment of complete silence. Standing in the doorway was a dark-haired smallish woman dressed in a bright green raincoat. Her face, somewhat obscured in the dim light, was wreathed in a friendly smile.

"Come in, come in," Theo said, wheeling himself backward and turning himself back to the room. "We have a visitor. Morgan and Clay Ashton, I want you to meet Mrs. Claire Simmons."

Chapter 8

The Book

On the afternoon of October 28, with the sky filled with scudding clouds and the windshield spotted with rain, the Ashtons were again on the road, motoring south from Oxford, their destination the Georgian market town of Petersfield. Clay, his hands firmly clenched on the steering wheel was driving. Morgan, using the magnifying glass she had borrowed from Theo, was quietly studying the road map that lay half unfolded in her lap.

Satisfied that her directions had allowed them to navigate the dreaded roundabouts around Winchester without mishap, Morgan refolded the map and placed it in the black leather briefcase that sat at her feet. For several minutes they rode in silence savoring the crisp, damp air that bathed their faces through the partially opened car windows.

A chain of low chalk hills, obscured from time to time by dense clumps of beech trees, their leaves tinged in bright gold, bordered a lane-like highway that the petrol station attendant said meandered a bit, but would eventually take them east to Petersfield without the distress of heavy traffic.

Morgan, whose eyes had been absently following a line of lichen covered low stone walls that edged the road, finally broke the silence.

"Tell me again what you thought of Mrs. Simmons," she

said, turning and giving Clay a searching look. "Until I took her hand, I really didn't think she existed."

"I guess I didn't either," Clay said, pushing the button that closed the windows. "I'd say though that she hadn't changed much from the description the grocer's wife gave me back at Stratford. She's still a bit on the heavy side and she still wears her hair pulled back in a pug."

"Did you notice her eyes, Clay? They looked almost translucent. At first I had the peculiar sensation that we had met before; it may have been her voice, but there was something about her that seemed familiar."

"To be honest, I almost dropped my brandy when Leonard answered the bell and announced that the caller was Claire Simmons. Did you notice how they both greeted her? Theo even tried to leave his wheelchair to give her a hug."

"Mmm, yes," Morgan replied, giving Clay a frowning look. "We talked about meeting Leonard for dinner some evening, but having him and Mrs. Simmons appear in Theo's office within an hour of each other...Clay, there is something strange going on here. The cottage at Stratford, the book that described those mysterious disappearances that I read to you, the painting of the pub over the fireplace and the people's faces that seemed to have been painted over, the scarab in the laquered box, the voices that I heard, the woman in the patio door, Alan Crabtree, the Beechams, the song *Greensleeves* coming from our cottage in Oxford, and now the appearance of Claire Simmons in Theo's office. These aren't accidental occurrences, Clay. They're linked somehow, but how and why?"

Morgan grew silent. Her forefingers pressed against her lips, she stared glassidly at the road ahead.

"I thought it odd that she never once mentioned the cottage at Stratford or asked how we enjoyed our stay there,"

Clay said, his voice taking on an unsettled tone. "I also thought it odd that she left so suddenly. I don't think I heard a reason, did you?"

"No, but I did feel she had come for some unexpressed purpose," Morgan said, shrugging her shoulders. "And I feel it was a purpose that all three of them shared."

"Well, we did find out that she operates a bed and breakfast in Morning Meadow and both Theo and Leonard had lodged with her during their field investigations there. And I did find her observations about dreams interesting," Clay said, giving Morgan a half smile.

"Yes," Morgan responded softly, her eyes still riveted on the road. "I was watching both Theo and Leonard as Claire told the story of her friend who dreamed he saw himself appear as a young boy in the same room where he was sitting and reading."

"I must have missed that part," Clay said, glancing down and adjusting the heater switch.

"That may have been when you made one of your frequent trips to the bathroom," Morgan said, giving Clay a sly glance.

"Brandy does that to me, you know."

"Yes, well, it was an interesting story. In his dream, the boy wore a knap sack which the man remembered he had often carried to school and, as they talked, long-forgotten scenes and events in his childhood began to appear. The boy showed him a bruise on his hand which the man remembered receiving as a consequence of falling out of a tree. Claire said that when her friend awoke, his pillow was wet with tears and every time he would think of his dream, his eyes would fill with tears. I think you were still out of the room when Leonard said that the dream proved his earlier point that the past and present do meld together in dreams. But what I found intriguing about the man's dream was that he appeared as a man and as a boy at the same moment in time."

"And what do you make of Claire's story?" Clay asked, giving Morgan an bemused look. "I don't believe I've ever encountered my double in my dreams, but the dream I mentioned earlier is so vivid it sometimes stays with me the entire day."

"Really? That's unusual." Morgan's eyes widened as she turned and gave Clay a thoughtful look.

"Yes, but before I describe it, I want your thoughts on Claire's story. I take it that you feel it's connected in some way to what we've already experienced."

"You are so perceptive, my dear," Morgan said, putting her hand on Clay's neck and turning in her seat so that one leg was under her. "I agree with Leonard about how time flows together in our dream states, but I'm not so sure that dreams that produce one's double are all that rare."

"Have you had such a dream?" Clay asked, his voice betraying the suspicion that she had.

"Yes." Morgan paused to shift her gaze back to the road ahead. "In a dream about a year ago, I saw myself as I am now and as a girl of about twelve. I was aware that I was asleep and that I was dreaming. The two of us sat in my aunt's colorful flower garden in Fincastle on a bright summer day and talked and talked about the present and the past. Oh, what memories she helped me revisit. I remember that both she and I sat there twirling the ends of my hair as we talked. I still do that. It was wonderful. Then about six months ago—it was April I think—I was sitting on a bench in front of the Old Main at Centre reading and enjoying the warm sun when I saw her, myself, as a girl again. That time she was running toward me in a way that I remembered myself doing when I got close to home after school. It lasted but a second or two and the vision was gone."

For a moment or two there was silence.

"You're twirling the ends of your hair," Clay remarked dryly, giving Morgan an amused look.

"Yes I am," Morgan said, giving Clay a peck on the cheek. "I'm sorry I got sidetracked, honey. You asked me for my thoughts about Claire's story."

"No, no I want to hear more about your encounter with yourself," Clay said, turning and taking her hand in his. "You said that when you saw yourself as a young girl, you were aware that you were asleep. Has the girl reappeared since?"

"No, she hasn't," Morgan began somewhat hesitantly. "But about a year ago...it was in late September and classes were about to begin, someone left a scuffy looking book on my desk. It was entitled, *A World Beyond Dreams* and the cover was so old and tattered that I couldn't help picking it up and paging through it. The author was a woman by the name of Jane Colwyn and the book was published in England at Cambridge in 1902."

"Interesting title," Clay said, giving Morgan a studied look.

"Yes, well, you know how hectic life can be just before a new school year begins. Well, I left it sitting on a nearby table along with dozens of others that I had received during the summer. I had forgotten it completely until one evening after a faculty meeting I went back to the office to pick up my appointment calender and found our cleaning lady, Mrs. Michem, standing near the table with the tattered book in her hands. She was facing me as I came in and she must have seen that I was somewhat startled because she said, 'I'm sorry, Mrs Ashton, I'm not one to snoop, but I couldn't help noticing this book'. I remember saying something about how it had mysteriously appeared on my desk and she was welcome to borrow it. I was a bit preoccupied with the thought of retrieving my calendar which was not where I thought I had left it.

As I was rummaging through the desk drawer in a mild state of panic I heard her say, 'No, Mrs. Ashton, this book is for you to read. It has your names inscribed on the back cover.' She handed me the book and our names were there, yours and mine, written in such a beautiful cursive hand that for a moment I completely forgot why I had gone back to my office. You haven't met Mrs. Michem, Clay, but she is similar in stature to Claire Simmons, and there is a kind of disarming amusement in her eyes."

"Is Mrs. Michem another one of these destined occurrences?" Clay asked, turning and giving Morgan a controlled smile. "And did you ask her if she was the one who had left the book on your desk?"

"No, but I did read the book and about two weeks after our meeting I met her again. I was working late when she came in. I remember looking up and smiling, and she nodded as she went about the business of dusting and emptying the waste baskets. Her voice is soft and I must not have heard her at first, but then I heard her say, 'Mrs. Ashton, I asked if you had read the book we talked about several weeks ago'. The tone of her question was so deliberate that I found myself putting aside the reports I had been reading. But before I could answer, she asked if I knew that she had lived in England before coming to the United States. I said I didn't and she said that she had lived many years in a village called Little Coxwell and still had friends living there. I asked if she had gone back for visits and she said she had many times, in her dreams."

"Can we continue this over lunch?" Clay asked, looking over his glasses. "I'm half starved and it's near one o'clock."

The small black and white rectangular sign anchored to an iron post read Dunston, and several sharp turns took them across a moss covered stone bridge onto a narrow village street tightly packed with quaint-looking shops.

"Can you tell us where we might find a restaurant?" Clay asked a woman who was standing under a dripping umbrella waiting for traffic to clear an intersection.

"Yes," she said with a smile. "Go two blocks straight ahead and right at the yellow and red stop sign and watch for children crossing."

Her directions brought them to a dormered, one-story, salmon-colored building. Red, curved awnings shaded four latticed, white-shuttered windows under which rested an equal number of colorful flower boxes. A huge, dark blue wooden tea pot with gold lettering hung over the half glass paneled door announcing that they had arrived at the *Pantry House*.

The wide polished wood floor creaked under foot as they were ushered by a hostess to a light oak rectangular table near a stone fireplace in which a crackling fire burned cheerily. The room had the warm, spicy smell of a bakery.

"Are you tired, honey?" Morgan asked, reaching across the table and taking Clay's hands in hers. "I don't think either of us slept well last night."

"No, I'm not tired—just hungry," Clay said, leaning across the table and giving Morgan a peck on the lips. "But after we eat I want to hear more about your dreams."

Their leisurely dinner over, Clay, after neatly refolding his napkin, joined Morgan on her side of the table facing the fire.

"We need to use our own fireplace more," Clay said, his eyes fixed absently on the fire. "There is something about a fire on a rainy day,"...his voice trailed off.

Morgan didn't answer. Her eyes too were riveted on the fire that popped and crackled.

"Let's continue our talk about dreams," Clay said, taking a deep breath. "How would the English phrase it? Continue straightaway or something like that."

"Your requests, my dear, are quite irresistible," Morgan responded, giving Clay a peck on the cheek while their attentive waitress refilled their cups with steaming tea.

Morgan ran her thumb over the raised flower design on her tea cup. "Well, where should I begin? The book, yes, the book. You know how children fantasize? Well, ever since I was little, and especially when I became bored in school, I would have these wonderful daydreams about this place...I'm sure now it was in England where time seemed to stand still. While there were older people in this place, I never seemed to grow any older, although somehow I knew that the world beyond my daydreams continued to grow older. Seems strange, doesn't it?"

"No, no," Clay said, peering over his tea cup. "I've had similar dreams or daydreams, but don't stop."

"Well," Morgan continued, her eyes taking on an unfocused look as they shifted toward the fire, "I would dream of this village with thatched cottages and cozy-looking shops nestled among towering trees. There was a meandering river crossed by ancient lichen-covered bridges in my daydreams. We would spend hours canoeing on the river and every so often we would pack a basket and picnic among the wild flowers in a nearby farmer's field."

Holding her tea cup in both hands, she closed her eyes.

"Where are you?" Clay asked, taking the cup from her and gently setting it down.

"The people in the village were so kind and gentle," Morgan said smiling, her eyes still closed. "We would spend our evenings chatting, reading, going to band concerts, or just sitting outside enjoying the soft air. There was always music in the evenings. I remember," Morgan said, opening her eyes, "how we would spend hours watching fireflies cast their sparkles of light in the darkness. Everyone had a garden and the air was always perfumed with the sweet fra-

grance of flowers. Our cottage, which was thatched and covered with clinging roses, looked out on a cobblestone road
which wound its way around the village. There were always
strollers and the sounds of horses' hooves on the road, but I
never saw a car."

"Tell me about your 'we'," Clay said, placing his arm on
the back of Morgan's chair. "I take it that you were sharing
your daydreams with someone."

"I did," Morgan replied, taking a long sip of tea and giving Clay a searching look. "Honey, do you remember when
I told you that I had spent years searching for you? I knew
you were out there somewhere, you were in my dreams
both day and night. I created you and I knew you existed
somewhere. You were always with me and I knew I would
find you someday."

For a moment, the only sounds were the murmuring
voices of a dozen or so people seated at nearby tables and an
old fashioned cash register being rung near the door. As
Morgan spoke, Clay's eyes had been fixed on the contents of
his tea cup. When he finally looked up, Morgan could see
that her words had touched him deeply.

"Honey," Clay began, then stopped. It was evident that
he wanted to choose his words carefully. "First, I've never
met Mrs. Michem, but one day, now that you mentioned
it—it was well over a year ago—I found a letter from her on
my desk. It had come with the office mail. In the note, she
said she would be leaving a book on your desk entitled *Beyond Dreams* and that I should read it, but not divulge the
fact that she had placed it there. She also said in her brief letter that we would be visiting England within the next several
years. I wonder how she knew that? And that our dreams
would be realized in ways that we never thought possible.
There was no return address on the letter and I threw it in
the trash. Then when you said you created me and that you

knew we would find each other someday, I knew I had to tell you about the note. I'm sorry I didn't mentioned it before. I guess at the time I simply thought it was one of those crank letters we sometimes receive."

For a long moment they studied each other. Clay gently brushed Morgan's hair back from her cheek.

"What's going on, honey?" Clay half-whispered in a tone that betrayed both excitement and discomfort. "When you brought the book home I wanted to tell you, but why I didn't, I don't know. I'm reading it for the second time and I still don't think I'm making all the connections. It's funny that we haven't really talked about it until now. And there is this recurring dream I've had for years that I mentioned in the car. Honey, does all this makes sense?"

"No, it doesn't," Morgan said, picking absently at the last of her beef casserole. "Somehow I knew that Mrs. Michem had put the book on my desk. But there are several more dreams that I want to tell you about. You remember I told you about my visit to the records office in Stratford and that I had found a reference to a John Barnett who had emigrated to the Virginia Colony back in the middle of the 1700s? Well, since then I've had several dreams in which I have seen him standing next to a standing stone with strange markings on it."

"How do you know he's John Barnett?" Clay interrupted.

"I just know. The stone is about three feet high and has a blue cast to it. Each time I've seen him, I have gotten the feeling that somehow he and that stone are connected in some way with all these mysterious happenings."

"Several things that Mrs. Simmons said made me think she had also read the book or one similar to it," Clay said, glancing at the check that the waitress had just left. "I don't believe it's common knowledge that through training, Buddhists in Tibet are able to materialize anything they wish and can travel great distances without the aid of some form of physical locomotion."

"Nor do I," Morgan agreed, nodding her head. "I've never heard the book referenced in any conversation that I've had over the years except this last Monday in Theo's office. Yes, Claire, as well as Leonard and Theo, seemed quite familiar with the work. I did think, however, that their views were somewhat contrary to Jane Colwyn's in that they believed that controlled dreaming, as she referred to it, could be attained without much practice and that almost anyone who has longed to escape into a world of their dreams could do so."

"Ah, controlled dreaming—now there's a term that requires a bit of dissection," Clay said, half-standing and reaching in his back pocket for his wallet. "Your best professorial definition please. You know your brilliance is only exceeded by your beauty."

Morgan watched as Clay's exaggerated sober look slowly dissolved into an impish grin.

"You are an outrageous flatterer, my dear," Morgan said, half-laughing, "but modesty keeps me from agreeing with you... entirely, that is."

"I know it would," Clay replied with mock solemnity, and after looking at each other for a brief moment, they both burst into gales of laughter.

Their tearful convulsions immediately drew the attention of the surrounding patrons, who watched the breakup with an air of reserved amusement.

"Would you like more tea?" their waitress asked, smiling; her hand holding the steaming, brown tea pot trembled slightly as she posed the question.

"Yes, thank you," Morgan said, wiping her eyes.

"And you, sir?" she asked, holding the tea pot above Clay's cup.

"No, no thank you," Clay replied, giving the waitress a look of polite attention. "But don't you think I've married the most beautiful woman in the world?" he asked, taking Morgan's hand and kissing it.

"I most certainly do, sir. You two have lightened up this old room considerably and I hope you'll come back."

"We will try," Morgan said, taking a sip of her tea and giving the woman a warm smile.

"And now, my dear, after we have made a ridiculous spectacle of ourselves and thoroughly disrupted the propriety of this delightful restaurant, I want you to give me, as you promised, your thoughts about controlled dreaming," Clay said, drawing a deep breath.

"Did I promise?" Morgan asked, holding her tea cup in both hands and peering amusingly at Clay over the lip of the cup.

"Yes," Clay responded, taking out his hankerchief and wiping his nose. "You know my nose always drips when we laugh like that."

"I know." There was a pause as Morgan set down her cup and shifted her gaze toward a nearby window that was dressed in egg white lace curtains. A smile creased her lips. "Many of my hardened colleagues at Centre would no doubt find the book lacking in what is commonly referred to as dispassionate research and incisive observation and, therefore, would judge it interesting, but largely fanciful. But that aside, Jane writes with the passion of a believer, and what I feel is so beautifully presented is her belief that we can, with help, learn to experience the wonders of controlled dreaming. In other words, when I'm dreaming and I'm fully aware that I'm dreaming, I have the power, according to Jane, to bring anything into existence that I wish."

Morgan was conscious that Clay's eyes had shifted away from her and were fixed on the fire.

"You asked me what I thought," Morgan continued, lightly touching Clay's hand.

"Yes," Clay replied in a voice just above a whisper. "Do you agree with Claire that in a controlled dream state we can access other realms, create our own Shangri-las, enter what we create and if we wish, never to be seen again? I was watching Claire intently and, for a moment or two during her visit, I thought she had left us. Consciously she was with us, unconsciously she was somewhere else."

"She probably was, and yes, I agree with her completely," Morgan said, giving Clay a thoughtful smile. "Remember on the airplane we talked about the existence of realms or dimensions that our senses as yet have not penetrated? You made the comment that our minds are not prisoners of our senses. Well, we both know that images are more powerful than words. It would follow then, that we not only can create our own Shangri-Las or places of perfect happiness, fulfillment, and contentment through imagery, either while awake or asleep, but that these realms may, in turn, send out beacons or signals to guide us there."

"You actually believe that it's possible to disappear, vanish into a heaven-like creation?" Clay asked searchingly, holding his cup aside while their attentive and thoroughly fascinated waitress, who had been listening, filled it with steaming tea.

"We can either visit or we can take up permanent residence, whatever we prefer. And we in our Shangri-la can appear at any age that appeals to us."

"And who, my dear, sends out the signals?" Clay asked, replacing his searching look with a teasing smile.

"I don't know, possibly masters or guides from other realms or dimensions."

"And who, besides ourselves, reside in these self created realms?"

"I believe there is an invisible cord that ties certain people together, people who yearn for or are driven by the same desires. Don't ask me how or why, I just feel that there is."

"Can we exist in both worlds at the same time," Clay asked. "In other words, can I go to work as usual on a Monday morning, say hello to my secretary and simultaneously dwell in my Shangri-la, as you call it?"

Morgan pressed her forefinger against Clay's nose. "That question, my dear, is one we'll ask Claire Simmons when we get to Morning Meadow."

A cold, slanting rain driven by a stiff East wind continued to beat a steady tatoo on the windshield as they turned onto High Street in Petersfield. The car was snug and warm. Morgan had taken off her white socks and shoes that had gotten thoroughly soaked in their dash for the car and placed them under the car's heater. Now only slightly damp, she was in the process of reattaching them when she spotted the swinging signboard reading *Archibald Duncannon Bookseller* through her window that was partially steamed.

"I'll drop you, honey," Clay said, slowly edging his way through a somewhat narrow street lined on both sides with rain spatttered parked cars. "It's three o'clock now and if I'm not back in an hour or so, send a bobby after me."

Morgan nodded. Opening the door, she gave Clay a quick peck on the cheek and watched him disappear down the darkening, rain-soaked street.

Morgan's gaze strayed briefly to the overhead signboard which, buffeted by a sudden gust of wind, swayed violently producing a creaking, chilling sound.

Why are we here, and why am I feeling as if something strange and bizarre awaits us here, Morgan asked herself, as she pressed her hand against the brass door handle. *I sometimes feel more than I fully understand*, she said softly to herself. *I can't blame myself for thinking that our entire time in England has been theater-that Clay and I are players in some inscrutable play.* A streak of lightning followed by a clap of thunder, startled her and she suddenly felt wet and chilled.

A bell hanging from a brass hook over the door tinkled melodiously as she pushed open the windowless, heavy oak door. To her front was a long corridor-like room lined from floor to ceiling with books. A latticed window facing the street, and two large bay windows to the rear, cast a gray light on the bookshelves nearest them. Above, four large globe lights, hanging by long, pipe-like stems from the cracked plaster ceiling added a bit of welcome illumination to what Morgan felt was a gloomy and cheerless interior. The room was eerily silent, except for the loud ticking of an old fashioned kitchen clock resting on a table near the door.

"Can I help you?" a man asked in measured tones as he climbed down a traversing wooden ladder cradling several books in his right arm. Placing the books on a waist-high shelf that separated the upper and lower book cases, he reached for a stout bone-handled cane.

"Is there a book that you are looking for?" he asked, and with a sudden turn, he began to walk slowly toward the back of the room. Morgan noticed that he limped badly.

"Yes,' Morgan replied, taking a deep beath. Theo Weeks suggested that we stop to say hello and brouse in what he described as the most complete rare book collection in all of England."

"And your name?" the man asked, stopping and slowly turning.

"Morgan Ashton. My husband was kind enough to drop me off while he parked the car. We drove down from Oxford and are on our way to Morning Meadow."

"I know," the man said as he hobbled unsteadily toward Morgan. "Theo rang me up this morning to say I might expect you and your husband this afternoon. My name is Archibald Duncannon. Theo has a propensity for exaggerating my collection because he considers rare books an intriguing novelty. I can offer you and your husband a cup of tea as soon as he arrives, but in the meantime, please hang your raincoat on the tree just around the corner of that bookcase."

The man, as he leaned on his cane and set a blue enameled kettle atop an ancient looking hot plate, appeared tall and somewhat stooped. His eyes seemed grey behind his horn-rimmed spectacles that rested well below the bridge of his aquiline nose. His long, narrow, clean-shaven face, his black hair, bushy eyebrows, high cheekbones and thin blue lips, gave his face a decidedly emaciated appearance. The clattering of his cane striking the flagstone floor echoed through the room.

"I'm sorry if the noise startled you," Archibald said, his voice betraying his annoyance. "An unruly cane can be one of life's uncertain allies."

"I know, my uncle walked with a cane," Morgan said, picking it up and leaning it against the table. "He was wounded by a German shell fragment, which smashed his leg. Were you hurt in the war?"

"Yes." In an attempt to retrieve his cane, Archibald's toe caught the leg of the table and he lurched sideways, his face contorted in pain.

"I'm sorry," Morgan said nervously as she helped him steady himself. "I should have placed the cane within reach."

"And so you did," Archibald responded, straightening himself by placing his hand on Morgan's arm. "I'm afraid that for many of my generation, the war authored many a chronic misfortune. Our sometimes reluctant reflexes seem to be the most noticeable. But we hold no bitterness. Liberty extracts a price."

The jangling of the bell disturbed the brief moment of silence that followed. Clay, his hands busily flapping his dripping raincoat, stood in the doorway with his rain soaked hair matted to his head.

"Beastly day, just beastly," he said with an impish grin as he wiped his face with his hankerchief.

"I assume this is Mr. Ashton?" Archibald asked, turning and flipping the electric switch on the hot plate.

"A very wet Mr. Ashton, I may add," Morgan said, helping Clay off with his raincoat.

At Archibald's direction, Morgan and Clay seated themselves in two overstuffed and threadbare chairs in a windowless room behind several tall free standing bookcases. The heat from a small electric fireplace and the steaming cups of tea that Archibald set before them helped to dispell the damp chill that had infiltrated the bookstore.

"Theo tells us that you have done considerable research into the lore that surrounds ley lines and standing stones," Morgan said, studying Archibald intently while placing her hand on Clay's knee. There was a creaking sound as Archibald settled himself in an uncomfortable straight-backed, spindled, wooden chair.

"Yes, they are subjects that must be approached with some delicacy," Archibald replied, stretching his damaged leg out before him. "They're topics in which facts skirmish with fancy."

Both Morgan and Clay smiled.

"We fully understand," Clay said, giving Morgan a faint smile. "We'll be driving on to Morning Meadow tomorrow. Can you give us a bit of background on what we will see?"

"Many of the standing stones have been pulled down and now form the walls of nearby cottages," Archibald said, taking a sip of tea and returning Clay's steady gaze. "But there are enough still in place so that one can imagine what the original complex looked like."

"Theo said that you're not obedient to accepted traditions regarding ley lines and standing stones and that you hold some unconventional views on the genesis of those at

Morning Meadow," Morgan said, leaning forward and placing her cup and saucer on a small table in front of her.

"I'm sorry, but I will have to close shortly," Archibald said abruptly, taking a gold watch out of his vest pocket and flipping open the cover. "But briefly, my assumption is that each standing stone complex has its own unique purpose. There are those that possess the power to heal, there are others that bring good fortune, there are still others that incite fertility and fecundity. Morning Meadow, I believe, possesses special magical powers. Theo is right. I'm not obedient to the current scholarly explanations and theories. I believe that at one time, there was at Morning Meadow a circle of blue stones, a few of which still exist, that possess mysterious powers that allow persons to enter parallel realities or worlds of their own choosing."

Noticing that Clay had given Morgan a brief, but questioning look, Archibald leaned forward as if to drive home his point.

"These worlds, I may add, are not illusionary, but are populated by people, animals, flowers, trees, houses, that are just as real as anything that we experience in the here and now. The blue stones act as gates into these parallel worlds and are scattered throughout England as well as the rest of the world. Those who have been longing and searching for a personal reality that embodies peace, contentment, and fulfillment and are willing to give up the trappings of our so called modern society, with its emphasis on power, prestige, and self-interest, may, through some mysterious force, discover the power of these blue stones. If and when they do, the choice to enter is theirs."

"How were these stones carried to other parts of England and to the rest of the world?" Morgan asked in a soft voice, her eyes riveted on her host.

"I believe they were carried by those who were associated

with the original purpose of the stones, masters if you will. Over the eons, they reincarnated and in the process carried and repositioned the stones to form gates to worlds that we thought only existed in our dreams. Why do you ask?"

The question would go unanswered. The sudden sharp ringing of the doorbell announced that the bookstore had another visitor. Glancing toward the door, Morgan caught her breath. Standing in the doorway closing a dripping, black umbrella was the man that Morgan thought she had seen leaning against the gate alongside the road between Swallow Falls and Oxford. She remembered that he had commented about how the village that lay far down the valley received very little rain. For a long moment, she studied him intently. When he looked up, she noticed he was blind.

Chapter 9

The Stones

"Oh, what a beautiful day," Morgan sighed. The dark, lowering clouds of yesterday had drifted off to the east, leaving the unfenced, camel-back hillsides, carpeted with purple heather, bathed in bright warm sunshine. Slowly wheeling and fluttering over the low bushes that lined the narrow blacktopped road were dozens of brown sparrow-like birds.

"What kind of bird is that?" Clay asked, slowing and opening his window. "I don't think I've heard a bird sing quite like that."

"Skylarks, I believe," Morgan said, lowering her window. "They do sing beautifully."

"Coffee, honey?" Morgan asked, as she held a steaming thermos over two white insulated cups.

Clay nodded. "That man who entered the bookstore just as Archibald was ready to close gave you quite a start didn't he?" Clay asked, giving Morgan a frowning look.

"Yes, he did. He looked for all the world like the man we saw standing at the gate gazing down that wonderfully peaceful looking valley. Although the man at the bookstore was blind, the resemblance was uncanny."

"I just got a brief look at him so I can't help you much," Clay said, giving Morgan a warm smile. "Archibald couldn't have missed your surprised look. He was just getting up when the man arrived and, given the British propensity for courtesy, I thought it odd that he didn't introduce us."

"So did I," Morgan replied.

As they headed north from the ancient Roman town of Salisbury with its magnificent towering cathedral, fleecy clouds the color of whipped cream began to appear over the undulating and treeless expanse identified on the map as Salisbury Plain.

"What a lonely and mysterious place," Morgan said, half to herself, her eyes fixed on the road ahead. "It feels as if someone or something is watching us. It must be a terribly dreary place when it rains."

I'm not very good company for Clay, Morgan said to herself as she turned and put her arm across Clay's shoulders. She had expected their visit to England to be unusually different, but what she and Clay had experienced in the past few days had left her drained and shaken. It was after three when she finally fell asleep last night. Her thoughts kept returning to the cottage at Stratford and the frightening sounds that only she had heard. The woman standing in the patio door. Had she been with them in the cottage for the entire time? The thought made her shiver. And the sound of music coming from their cottage in Oxford the night they arrived. Everything that has happened to us has had some purpose. But what? What was it that Leonard had said when she told him she had decided to spend her sabbatical in England? 'Yes,' she remembered him saying, 'you and Clay will no doubt discover many strange and possibly distressing events, but in the end I'm sure that both of you will experience a peace and contentment that you never thought possible.' Deep in thought, Morgan was faintly conscious that her hands felt cold and that she was rubbing them together.

"Are you cold, honey?" Clay asked, giving Morgan a questioning look.

"I'm sorry if I left you for a moment," she said, giving Clay an embarrassed smile. "But yes, you know my hands and feet are always cold."

"Do we want to stop at Stonehenge?" Clay asked, taking Morgan's hand. "I think we're close."

"No, Mrs. Simmons said she would have lunch waiting for us and it's nearly eleven o'clock now. But, let's resume our talk about Morning Meadow's blue stones. Archibald's views were certainly unusual; at least I've never heard or seen them expressed before."

"Nor I. Do you actually think he's stumbled across some ancient, mystical secret, or do you think he is the type of person the English refer to as balmy? He's certainly eccentric."

"He's not balmy," Morgan said, giving Clay a sudden flashing glance, "but there is a touch of eccentricity about him. When he referred to the blue stones as gates to other worlds, I remembered a dream I had, just the night before in which I saw this man, I felt it was John Barnett, standing beside a blue stone...I wonder."

"I thought that his comment about the world ending when those blue stones are returned to Morning Meadow was a bit of a stretch. I don't remember him saying how that suprising bit of prophesy was obtained."

"It's not suprising," Morgan remarked, giving Clay a look of feigned innocence. "You were in the bathroom."

Clay at that moment had been taking a sip of coffee and in his eagerness to reply, opened his mouth. The result was that several drops of warm liquid ran down his chin. Morgan, expecting some sort of sardonic reply, quickly produced her handkerchief and caught the dribbles before they reached his grey sweater.

"Coffee does that to me."

"I know," Morgan replied, returning Clay's broad grin with an impish smile.

For a dozen or so miles they rode in silence. The uneven ground of the Plain had given way to chains of green, carpeted, low chalk hills dotted here and there by grazing sheep. In the passing miles, the cotton-like clouds had also drifted east to be replaced by long stands of whispy clouds that seemed frozen against a sky of delicate blue.

"Tell me about the return of the stones to Morning Meadow," Clay said, giving Morgan a furrowed look.

"Yes, the stones," Morgan said, turning and resting her back against the door. "Well, Archibald said that several years ago he had successfully bid on a number of rare books at an estate sale in Bath. In one of the books he found several sheets of folded paper that he thought had been separated from a larger sheaf or manuscript. He said that the sheets were so old and brittle that parts of them crumbled as he attempted to unfold them. The once-original black ink, he said, had turned to a faded brown, but he was able to discern that the author was a person, probably a monk or an abbot known as Peter of Whitby. There was no date, but a subsequent investigation established that an Abbey by the name of Whitby did exist near Bath in the ninth century. The sheets, of course, are not original and he doesn't know who the copier was or when the copying was done." Morgan stopped and reached for her coffee. "Interesting, honey?" she said, eyeing Clay over the top of the cup.

Clay nodded.

"Well, to continue, the monk or abbot, writing in Latin had related how a people living near circles of standing stones believed that a particular circle of blue stones, the ones that Archibald believes stand at Morning Meadow, had the power to affect their minds in such a wonderous manner that they could mysteriously disappear from their village and could return whenever they wished. He wrote how his brothers had tried to minister to these people, but their leaders said that a great spirit had already made a sacred trust with them and had shown them the wonders of unseen creations. They also believed that when the stones, which had been mysteriously carried off, are returned to their places, everything around them would disappear forever."

Nestled in a fold of the grass carpeted low lying hills and stretching along a meandering mirror-like river that Morgan had identified as the Stour lay a scattering of honey-colored cottages their tar-colored thatched roofs all but obscured by stands of trees whose leaves had turned to a rusty brown and a faded yellow. At the bottom of a gently-descending curve a blue sign with white letters anchored to a black iron post announced that they had arrived at Morning Meadow.

"What an interesting name," Morgan said as she closed the road atlas and tucked it away in her brief case. "We'll have to ask Mrs. Simmons how it came to be."

Crossing a lichen-encrusted single-arched stone bridge that spanned the sparkling waters of the glasslike river, the narrow road, canopied by ancient oaks and elms, curved round a small green fronted by several cozy looking cottages upon whose brittle and scaly looking grey slate roofs grew tufts of green moss.

A man wearing a flat cap, tweed jacket and knickers and walking a collie waved as they passed him.

"What a glorious fall day," Morgan sighed, as she pressed the switch that lowered the window a bit. "Autumn, the smell of burning leaves, I love it."

Mrs. Simmons' directions had been quite specific. Primrose, as she referred to her bed and breakfast, was one of five, pale limestone homes that bordered the village's most picturesque attraction, its duck pond.

"She writes," Morgan said, scanning Mrs. Simmons' letter, "that there are several old oaks to the rear of her house and a flagstone walk leads to an amber-colored door enclosed by a rose arbor. The roof is a reddish orange tile with two fluted chimneys on each end. If she's not at home, she says we should make ourselves comfortable, the door will be unlocked and, if we're hungry, there will be sandwiches and milk in the refrigerator, as well as hot coffee on the stove.

"I wonder if her house was once a mill?" Morgan asked, as she got out of the car and slowly started down a flower-bordered gravel path that curved around the side of the building.

The sun-bathed limestone felt warm to the touch and for the moment, dispelled the slight chill that she felt. At the rear of the house, hidden by hawthorne hedges and a red brick wall that faced the river, was a garden filled with fall blooming flowers and arbors covered with yellow, pink and red roses. For a moment, Morgan stood transfixed at the beauty of her discovery.

"The front door is this way," Clay called as he pulled the suitcases from the trunk and closed it with a thud. "Do you want your briefcase?"

"Yes," Morgan replied, somewhat absently as she wandered back, her arms wrapped around her. "There's a feeling of peace and serenity here," she said, taking her briefcase from Clay. "Isn't that interesting? Is that a sprig of mistletoe chiseled in the stone block over the door?"

Clay, his arm cradling their jackets and his hands clenching two overnight suitcases, looked up. "So it is. Do you think Claire would mind if we steal a kiss on her doorstep? It must be an ancient English custom."

"And...a custom we shan't ignore," Morgan said softly, setting her briefcase aside and throwing her arms around Clay's neck.

The voices drifting down the long hallway sounded familiar. Standing in the far doorway was Leonard, and to his side with a sandwich in his hand was Theo, his face enveloped in a wide smile.

"Come in, come in," Leonard said, beckoning, "the kitchen is the coziest place in these old piles." Morgan and Clay exchanged surprised glances. "Theo and I spent the weekend nosing about the circle. We were about to leave, but agreed with Claire that we should stay long enough to say hello."

"She trooped off to the market about a half hour ago," Theo said, wheeling himself forward. "It's good to see both of you again."

Clay, draping their coats over the banister that led to the second floor, grasped Leonard's and Theo's outstretched hands.

"We didn't see a car," Morgan said, giving each a hug.

"No," Theo said, laying his sandwich on the table. "Leonard parked on the other side of the duck pond so as not to raise your suspicions. But come and sit down. Claire's prepared chicken salad sandwiches and poppyseed cake and she would be miserably disappointed if we did not partake."

"Before entering, we noticed the sprig of mistletoe cut into a stone over the door. We wondered if it was a signature stone of the builder," Clay said while pulling a spindled-backed chair back for Morgan.

"I don't believe so," Theo replied, setting the brakes on his wheelchair. "Mistletoe was considered a holy plant by the Druids or Celtic priests. It supposedly was used in many of their rituals and represented the end of the old and the beginning of the new."

"Did you stop at Petersfield?" Leonard asked somewhat idly as he carefully poured steaming tea into the waiting cups.

"Yes, were you able to secure Hillary Bowden's book?" Theo asked, while retrieving his sandwich. "And what were your impressions of our estranged friend?"

"Estranged?" Morgan repeated, giving Clay a surprised look. "Yes, Archibald found a copy of Hillary's book for us, but what do you mean estranged?"

"His hypothesis about blue stones here at Morning Meadow and how they are thresholds to other realities has provoked a great deal of criticism among ley hunters and students of the stones," Leonard said, while slowly stirring a teaspoon of sugar into his cup.

"Yes," Theo agreed, "Archibald has become somewhat of a private embarrassement to a number of his colleagues in the rare book business who publicly state that the papers he found are a fictitious fake. Part of the problem stems from his decision not to allow a scholarly examination of the manuscript or have it carbon dated."

"I take it you both have seen the manuscript?" Morgan asked, looking up after slicing the bulging cellophane-wrapped sandwich in half. "And may I ask if you both accept Archibald's hypothesis about the blue stones?"

The questions would go unanswered. The heavy oak kitchen door opened with a decided squeak.

"I"m happy to see that Leonard and Theo are making you feel right at home," Claire said, as she brushed back a wisp of hair and placed her market basket on the cabinet counter. "The grocers was a bit crowded and it took longer than I expected. It's so wonderful to see you both," she continued, strolling over and giving both Morgan and Clay a hug. "I suppose Theo and Leonard have been boring you with stories of Morning Meadow and our legendary stones?"

"Well yes," Clay said after a brief pause, "but we didn't get to hear how Morning Meadow got its name. The name fits so wonderfully with the landscape."

"Quite so," Claire said, looking up after emptying the contents of her basket. "Both Theo and Leonard can attest to the fact that appearing in the Domesday Book is the name Moaning Stones, a hamlet of a dozen people situated near the remains of a circle of blue standing stones." Claire paused to slice herself a piece of cake. "Contrary to our reputation of being soberly reserved, we English are romantics who, by and large, find legend and tradition much more interesting and comforting than scientific determinism."

Claire's brief glances at both Theo and Leonard were met by amused looks and extravagant noddings by both men.

"During the middle of the 17th century, the name was changed," Claire continued, "to Morning Meadow, but tradition persists that on certain nights, especially during the full moon, one can hear the stones utter a low moaning wail."

"Have *you* heard such a moan?" Morgan asked softly.

"Yes."

The sudden raspy sound of the old fashioned crank-type door bell interrupted further discussion of Claire's terse response. Appearing in the latticed kitchen door window was a smiling, somewhat rotund woman with cinnamon colored hair.

"Come in, come in, Abigail," Claire called, getting up and pressing the handle that unlatched the door. "What in the world?"

"Now, now dear," Abigail said, depositing two pies in Claire's outstretched hands and rubbing her hands on her flowered apron. "I thought your guests might enjoy a freshly-baked apple rhubarb and a pear pie. I hope you like them," she said, smiling.

"You know Leonard and Theo of course," Claire said, escorting Abigail to the table. "And I want you to meet my American friends, Morgan and Clay Ashton. Abigail is the wife of our vicar, Patrick Puffington."

"He's Paddy to everyone in Morning Meadow," Abigail said, smiling as she took Morgan and Clay's hand.

"We saw the spire of a church just visible over a neighboring hill," Morgan said, moving her chair to make room for the one that Claire had retrieved from across the room.

"That would be our St. Michael's, dear," Abigail said,

placing her chubby hand on Morgan's. "As you saw, it lies a bit of a walk from our village. Our Calvinist forebears felt that more than a modest effort was needed to attend church. Oh, bye the bye, Claire, I repaired the hem of your red robe so that you can wear it for the church service on Sunday."

"St. Michael's must be one of the last churches in England in which this custom persists," Leonard said, giving Abigail an amused look while helping himself to a vanilla-frosted square of poppyseed cake.

"What custom is that?" Clay asked, solemnly following Leonard's lead.

"It's a tradition going back hundreds of years that members wear a red robe in church," Claire said.

"Yes," Abigail said with a sigh. "It's most reassuring that a few of the our valued ecclesiastical customs have survived the casual familiary that has overtaken our churches. We wear our robes, Mr. Ashton, to cover our vanity. No one is dressed any more stylishly than anyone else."

"Speaking of stylish," Morgan interjected, "I've been admiring the necklace you're wearing. It's a scarab, isn't it? May I take a closer look?"

Morgan had thought that their vexing experiences of the past several weeks had made her somewhat impervious to surprise, but the scarab hanging from a gold chain around Abigail's neck filled her with a chilling sensation. She was also faintly aware that Theo and Leonard had exchanged quick glances.

"Of course, my dear," Abigail said, smiling as she turned her chair to face Morgan. "I wear it every day even though it clashes with my attire as it no doubt does with my print dress and my flowered apron."

"It's almost identical to the one Clay and I found in a lacquered box at our cottage in Stratford. The color of yours, however, is different." Morgan raised the scarab and gently held it in the palm of her hand. "The one in the box was fashioned in crystal. Yours is a blue violet. It's wonderfully shaped and very beautiful."

"Thank you, dear," Abigail said in an approving voice. "It was my grandmother's and from what my mother told me, she wore it continuously, except when she went to bed."

At that moment, in the failing late afternoon light, Claire, whose absence had gone unnoticed, reentered the room.

"There's a cheery fire awaiting you in the library just down the hall," she said, smiling and taking up a position behind Clay's chair. "Bring your tea cups if you wish and the remains of the cake. I can't abide anyone in the kitchen while I prepare dinner. It's one of our absurdities that I must insist upon."

"As do I," Abigail said, getting up suddenly. "But I must be getting home. We have Bible study tonight. It's not terribly well-attended now that this horrid suffocating invention called television has come to Morning Meadow, but we must endure what we cannot cure. And I understand from Claire that you and Clay wish to visit the stone circles at night," she said, taking Morgan's hand in both of hers. "Dress warmly dears. Those old stones can give you the shivers even on a warm summer night." With a wave of the hand she was gone.

The crackling fire cast a warm glow on the dark polished paneling and the tall bookshelves that lined the walls of the library.

"Tis a cozy room," Theo said, giving the flaming logs a jab with an iron poker. "The house has central heating, but Claire prefers to keep the fires going. It dispells the dampness that is so common in these old stone houses."

"So we've heard," Morgan said, leaning forward on the love seat to allow Clay to position a pillow against the small of her back.

"How old would you say Abigail is?" Clay asked, leaning back and stretching his legs under the table.

"Abigail's age? Mmm, she's probably approaching 80, don't you think Theo?"

Theo, his eyes riveted on the fire, shrugged.

"That's hard to believe," Morgan said, giving Leonard a suprised look. "She's very beautiful and looks so young. Her skin was satin smooth, I didn't see a wrinkle; and her eyes... hazel, yes hazel. They seemed to radiate a kind of soothing energy."

"I particularly liked her turned-up nose," Clay interjected, his eyes shining with amusement. Morgan didn't answer, but placed her head on Clay's shoulder.

"You found Abigail's scarab necklace interesting, Morgan?" Theo asked softly as he turned away from the fire, his eyes fixed on the diamond-shaped window panes that looked out on the darkening front yard.

"I thought it somewhat odd that Abigail was wearing a scarab similar to the one we discovered at Stratford," Morgan said, "We assumed it belonged to Claire, but it may not."

"It does," Leonard intoned. "And I'd venture to say it's her most valued possession."

Suddenly Clay jumped up and hurried from the room. A moment later he reappeared, carrying the black lacquered box and a book.

"I hope Claire doesn't mind, but we couldn't help looking inside. There's also a card attached to the underside of the cover written in French."

"And could you translate?" Theo asked, shifting his gaze back to the fire.

"Not very well," Morgan replied, leaning forward.

Except for the crackling of the fire, the room grew quiet.

"And what is the name of the book you're holding, Clay?" Leonard asked, holding out his hand. "May I see it? Ah, Hillary Bowden's book. Are either of you familiar with her theories about color?"

"No," Morgan replied, "but we found her name in a

book that we discovered in our cottage at Stratford. The book—it seemed more like a manuscript—bore no title or publisher and it was written in the most beautiful handwriting I've ever seen. It described the mysterious disappearances of a number of people, including Hillary Bowden. Whoever made the entries said she taught Experimental Physics at Oxford and that later, while visiting some friends in Swallow Falls, we found Miss Bowden had written a book entitled, *Experimenting With Unseen Colors.*"

The room again grew silent. Theo continued to gaze at the fire, which was slowly being reduced to glowing coals. Leonard, leaning forward, was methodically paging through the book. With the waning fire, the room had become colder. Knowing how Morgan disliked being cold, Clay retrieved a multi-colored afghan from the back of a nearby rocking chair and placed it around her. Theo, too, sensing that the room had become chill, placed a large split log on the coals.

Theo broke the silence. "Hillary, besides being a respected physicist and an esteemed colleague, was an amateur botanist," he said, absently giving the log a poke with the pick-like iron. "Her fascination with color included flowers and about everything else in nature that absorbs and reflects light."

"Yes," Leonard said, handing the book back to Clay. "Botany was her first love. Floral designs and color patterns of plants intrigued her. Her apartment in Oxford was like a greenhouse filled with all manner of flowering plants and even trees. And didn't you tell me, Theo, that she had rented a plot outside of town, where she nutured and experimented with hundreds of species of wild and domestic plants?"

"A study that no doubt held much promise," Morgan remarked, offhandedly, drawing her legs under her. "But from the title of her book I assume she feels that current theories about light and color are in need of some modification."

"Precisely," Theo said, suddenly looking away from the fire and fixing Morgan with a steady look. "However, the book evoked a great deal of unfavorable commentary from reviewers who deemed her assumptions both fanciful and heretical."

"And what were her assumptions?" Morgan and Clay asked simultaneously, glancing at each other and smiling.

"Simply put," Theo continued, "colors that we encounter in our dream state are often much more vivid than what we observe during our waking state. Hillary postulated that our minds are capable of registering and sensing a much wider range of light waves with their corresponding range of colors and frequencies than science has led us to believe."

"What you have related so far seems plausible and certainly not worthy of the term heretical. There must be more," Morgan said, giving Leonard a vague smile.

"There is. Somewhere in the book she describes how, as a young girl she came across a tea rose growing alone and wild in a field near her home. Such an uncommon discovery, of course, required her full attention and she relates that as she examined it, she felt herself being drawn into it. She wrote that suddenly the rose opened and a world that she had experienced only in her dreams stretched out before her. The colors, she said, were much more vivid than anything she had ever seen. Overwhelmed by feelings of joy, peace and contentment, she says, she was about to enter the world of the rose when she heard her mother's call. She looked up for just a moment and when she looked back, the rose had disappeared. Had the rose really existed? She maintains that it had."

So engrossed were they in Theo's discourse that no one seemed aware that Claire had silently entered the room and was sitting in a rocking chair in the shadows just beyond the firelight in the otherwise darkened room.

"How does Hillary's interest in color relate to her experience with the rose?" Clay asked, leaning forward, folding his hands and resting his chin on his thumbs.

"Yes, is color somehow associated with one's ability to enter new realities or worlds?" Morgan added, slowly massaging Clay's shoulders.

"Partly." Clay felt Morgan give a little jump. "I'm sorry if I startled you," Claire said, pulling her rocking chair into the firelight. "But our sensitivity to color indeed plays an important role in helping us to see beyond our own reality."

"But how?" Morgan persisted, throwing off the afghan. "When I dream, I'm aware of not only color, but taste, smell, hearing, touch; all of my senses are active."

"As they should be," Claire replied, motioning to Theo to place another log on the fire. "The deep mind, or what some call the soul, along with everything else in nature, is made up of electromagnetic energy which physics tells us has no color, taste, or smell. It follows, then, that everything we see is merely what our senses interpret them to be: color, shape, feel and so on. Hillary's rose was a creation of her mind. But her creation was just as real and its color probably even more vivid than a tea rose one might see in a garden."

Morgan and Clay exchanged frowning glances.

"As you and Clay will see when you read the book, Hillary theorizes that there are many more colors in light than what we normally see. I believe in chapter eleven she describes how, in a dream, she became aware of colors that were more vivid and beautiful than anything she had ever encountered in her waking state. In her dream she found herself in a world not terribly different in appearance from our own. What was incredible and unforgettable was the overwhelming feeling of peace and tranquility she experienced."

Claire paused. The only sound was the crackling of the fire and the faint rustling of leaves caused by a sudden, sharp gust of wind. Leonard cleared his throat.

"Hillary wrote," Claire continued, her eyes fixed on Morgan, "that in her dream world, she taught botany at a college and she remembered that a sign over her office door read, 'Don't Underestimate One's Capacity For Usefulness No Matter Where You May Be.' The tea rose for Hillary was the first step toward accessing other worlds and realities. If one creates a rose, why not other objects and even dimensions that entertain, enthrall and excite one's interest? The possibilties are limitless. Our individual heavens lie within the mysterious realm of the mind and imagery is the key that unlocks the doors. But enough about Hillary for one evening," Claire said, getting up and motioning them to follow. "In Primrose House, dinner begins promptly at six. Afterwards we shall take our evening stroll."

A huge round harvest moon the color of burnished gold hung low in the eastern sky. The smell of burning leaves hung heavy in the hushed and soft evening air.

"Careful," Claire warned, playing her torch light from side to side. "The ground is terribly uneven and the rocks are sharp. We will be able to see the stones when we get to the top of this hill," she added, puffing a bit.

"It would be helpful to have a walking stick," Clay whispered, while tightly holding onto Morgan's arm. "Can't you picture us with our legs hanging in traction?"

"Yes," Morgan giggled. Except for the plaintive cry of a night bird and the voice of a mother calling her child home, the night was eerily quiet.

Just beyond the light of Claire's torch were the stones rising like ghostly sentinels against the light of the moon. Morgan caught her breath.

"It's not much further," Claire said, her puffing becoming more labored. "The tall stones ahead form what was once a great circle of fifty-six stones. The smaller blue stones form a separate and much more compact circle within the larger one. Originally there were twenty blue stones, two of which are still in evidence."

"Abigail and I often come here on nights when the moon is full," Claire continued, turning off her torch. "Especially when we become overly preoccupied with the day's distresses. We find in this ancient place a sense of unity and a feeling of balance and harmony with all things."

The night had became deathly still. There was no sound from the village below and the night bird had ceased its cry. Slightly below them in a slanting meadow lay the great circle of stones. Long shadows cast by the pale moon pointed like giant fingers toward the village which was slowly being enveloped by a low creeping fog.

Clay, who had put his arm around Morgan's waist, felt her shiver. "Are you cold?" he whispered, giving her a long, concerned look. "I must confess that I am."

Morgan shook her head. She could not explain how she felt. Fragments of thoughts flashed through her mind. Did the real purpose of their visit to England lay among these cold stones? she wondered. Suddenly, she felt herself overwhelmed by the uncanny and disquieting feeling that all her thoughts had vanished. For a long moment, she struggled to regain control. The thought that somehow she had lost touch with herself, for how long she didn't know, startled her. Faintly aware that Claire was speaking, she looked up to find Clay worriedly searching her face.

"I'm fine," she said, giving him a wan smile. "Just hold onto me."

"There is a path of sorts that leads around the outside of the larger circle, but I feel it may be too hazardous even, with the bright moonlight," Claire said. Gripping her torch and taking Morgan's hand while Clay held the other, she guided them down a series of rocky steps that led to the middle of the great circle.

"Wonder of wonders," Morgan half-whispered as they stood transfixed, surrounded by silent sentinels, several of which, framed in the pallid light of the moon, seemed to emit a strange metallic sheen.

"Am I the only one who's cold?" Clay asked, putting his

arm around Morgan's waist and pulling her toward him. "Honey, you're shivering too."

"Yes, but I'm not sure it's from the cold."

"What are you feeling?" Claire asked softly, taking Morgan's hand and rubbing it gently.

For a long moment there was silence.

"Clay...Clay," Morgan's voice sounded detached and far off. Her eyes were closed and Clay felt her stiffen. "Clay, I see."

"What do you see, honey?" Clay asked, his voice a mixture of excitement and alarm.

"Clay, the circle...the circle is like a...a...large round window. Oh, it's beautiful. The sun feels warm...a long valley with colorful wildflowers...a church spire...a... a...blue stone."

How long they had stood there, a half hour, an hour, Morgan didn't know. She was aware, however, that Claire had gently touched her shoulder.

"It's time to go back to the house," Claire said softly, putting her arm around Morgan.

Slowly, as if awakening from a deep sleep, Morgan opened her eyes.

"Where was I?" she whispered, her eyes searching Clay's face.

"We must be getting back," Claire said in a gently insisting tone. "I'll run the bath water and make you a hot cup of tea. We can discuss what you saw in the morning."

The rising, damp fog had all but obscured the duck pond and the houses that fronted it by the time they reached Primrose House. Claire, leading the way, had just opened the ancient iron gate in front of the house when they heard it—the low moaning sound coming from the direction of the great circle.

Chapter 10

The Photograph

Morgan quietly tiptoed down the winding staircase. The beeswax candle she carried cast flickering shadows on ancient family portraits hanging on the cracked plaster walls. Their eyes, devoid of expression, seemed to follow her and she wondered who among them had lived in Primrose House and how many of them had walked barefoot on these selfsame worn wooden stairs in the early morning.

Wrapping the heavy fleece robe that Claire had so kindly provided tightly around her, Morgan padded across the foyer to the music room, where a fire crackled and popped in a cavernous red brick fireplace. The golden glow of dawn filtering through the diamond shaped windows bathed the room in a warm and mellow light.

Three plush burgundy sofas formed a U around the fireplace and toward the back of the music room, surrounded by overstuffed chairs covered in flowery designs, stood a shiny black grand piano and a pedestal harp, whose taut strings were locked in a highly polished, arching frame of dark cherry.

Near one of the overstuffed chairs, a brown tea pot with a hint of steam rising from its snout rested on a small table, along with four cups and a cut glass bowl of sugar. Pouring herself a cup of steaming tea, Morgan continued to wander around the room, caressing the beautifully preserved instruments before sitting down on the thickly padded and delicately embroidered piano bench. Except for the crackling of the fire, the room was quiet. The faint smell of furniture polish teased her nostrils, and the ivory keys of the piano felt cold to her touch.

Paging through a yellowed and well-worn song book, Morgan stopped at one of her mother's favorites and gently smoothed the pages. The melodic sounds of *music* drifted softly around the room and down the long hallway that separated Claire's quarters from the music and formal dining rooms. Although she continued playing, she knew that someone had quietly entered the room. Leonard, she thought. He had, on many occasions, silently entered her office at Centre College, waiting for her to look up from her desk, always apologizing for the intrusion. Morgan rested her hands on her lap.

"Is that you, Leonard?" she asked, turning and smiling.

"Good morning, Morgan," Leonard nodded, pouring himself a cup of tea. "It's good to hear you play. Yes, you can almost feel the old house smile when someone sits down at the piano or the harp." There was a brief pause as he stirred a teaspoon of sugar into his cup. "But tell me about your visit to the stones," he continued, as he seated himself in one of the overstuffed chairs and crossed his legs.

Morgan smiled as she idly traced the lip of her cup with her finger. It was so like Leonard, she thought, to pose a question for which he already knew the answer. Did she have the words to describe how her very being had longed to experience the ecstasy she had felt last night?

"It was a wonderous, unforgettable evening, with the moon casting a silvery light on the stones," she said softly. "There is something truly revelational about this place. It's as if one can reach out to another realm, a place that you know exists, that you have seen, but only in your dreams. I felt restrained and unrestrained at the same time." Morgan paused. "I'm not doing a very good job of reporting, am I?" she asked, looking up and giving Leonard a wry smile.

"What do you mean you felt restrained and unrestrained at the same time?" Leonard asked, standing and placing his cup on the mirror-like piano top.

"When Claire guided us into the circle of large stones, I felt a tingling sensation and a bit dizzy. I closed my eyes and when I opened them, the sensations were gone and it was as if I was looking through a large window. What I saw was a beautiful scene of hillsides carpeted in purple and yellow flowers, of a village far off down a valley, of farmhouses nestled in the folds of gently-sloping hills. There were hedgerows and orchards. It was so peaceful and charming. I had this irresistible urge to step through the window, but somehow I felt restrained. I knew if I did, I may not have been able to return."

At that moment, Clay, dressed in jeans and a heavy, cream-colored knit sweater, popped his head around the corner.

"Oh, there you are," he said, giving Leonard a nod and giving Morgan a kiss on the top of her head. "Claire says that breakfast will be ready in twenty minutes."

"We've been talking about our adventure last night," Morgan said, looking up and smiling. "I was telling Leonard what I experienced while we stood in the circle."

For a long moment, no one spoke.

"What do you make of it, Leonard?" Clay asked, pouring himself a cup of tea. "I was alarmed...no, frightened is a better word. It was as if Morgan was about to leave her body. That I won't allow, not unless she takes me along," he said, smiling and taking a seat next to Morgan on the piano bench.

"What Morgan saw actually exists." Leonard said, making an indifferent gesture. "Our minds are indeed capable, in certain situations, of receiving and accurately processing such impressions when untroubled by outside influences.

Unfortunately," he continued, "such visions are often viewed as comforting illusions brought about by wistful thinking. At first, one may totally accept the vision of a world beyond ours and *become* eager to re-experience it. Later, it becomes subject to what Theo calls 'the principle of uncertainty'. Still later, as decisive explanations elude us, we tend to dismiss it altogether, thinking it scarcely conceivable or believable."

Stiffly rising from his chair, Leonard retrieved a split log from the woodbox and placed it on the fire. Caught in the blazing fire, Morgan noticed a wistfulness in his eyes.

"The potential for actually re-experiencing the vision that Morgan encountered," Leonard continued, poking absently at the fire blanketed logs, "lies in one's interest and capacity for revisiting the vision over and over. In so doing, one reinforces and builds on the thought patterns that in turn bring into existence that reality or realm that we long for. Thought is the most powerful force in the universe. As necessity is the mother of invention, so thought is the foundation of all creation."

"Suppose two people experience basically the same dreams and waking thoughts?" Clay asked, his voice betrayed the rising excitement that he was feeling. "Honey," he said turning to face Morgan, "I've been meaning to tell you about my recurring dream. You remember that picturesque valley you saw on our way to Oxford and how the man at the gate told us that the sun seems to shine there when the rest of the landscape is dripping? Well, while I didn't see what you saw, the scene you described was similar to the one that keeps recurring in my dreams." Clay was aware that Morgan's eyes had not left him since he began talking.

Suddenly her eyes filled and two large tears rolled down her flushed cheeks. Her heart pounded furiously and it took several seconds for her to fully understand her emotions. All along she had harbored the fear that the strange and eerie happenings they had experienced since their arrival in England had had some inexpressible purpose, a purpose that she would have to endure alone. Whatever else occurred they would experience it together. She closed her eyes and breathed a noticeable sigh. Faintly conscious that the room was quiet except for the crackling of the fire, Morgan opened her eyes to find both Clay and Leonard looking at her intently.

"You don't know how I have longed to hear you say that," she whispered, breathing a noticeable sigh and giving him a kiss on his cheek.

"The puzzle is not complete until we lay one of the last pieces in place," Leonard said gently, thoughtfully stroking his chin. "Attractive or unattractive as it may sound, I believe that there are people who share a single soul."

As he spoke, Morgan noticed that Leonard's eyes gleamed with a far and away look.

"Yes," he continued, "two people, a man and woman, sharing a common soul. Sometimes they choose to meet in a single lifetime and sometimes they don't. It's all part of a larger plan, a journey that they must share. It binds them together through all eternity. And part of their bonding is their capacity for experiencing the same feelings, thoughts, fears, and desires. Together their energies become so powerful that, with help from kindred spirits, they are able to penetrate other realms and worlds of their dreams. They can, if they choose, enter these realms and live forever in a state of perpetual bliss and contentment without the nasty habit of dying."

Except for the hissing of the dying fire, the room for a long moment was quiet.

"Some people who lack the genius for prose can, nevertheless, encourage it in others," Leonard continued, as he produced a ragged and somewhat worn piece of paper from his jacket pocket. "Years ago, a couple attended one of my classes who were very much in love. The Vietnam War was on and he was called into the Army. In class I had discussed my belief that two people could inhabit a single soul and they had confided that they had found a gentle comfort in the supposition. Several weeks after he had left, I found this piece of paper on my desk with a note from the woman directing me to read it. This is what she wrote:

'He waits for me beside the weathered flagstone path just inside our gate. We had planned it so before he went away. Like two flowers that bloom from a single stem we are separate, yet one. We have shared many lifetimes, he and I , and the love that binds us can never be severed by distance or death. I saw him the other day, although I know he is gone. I heard his voice. He beckoned me and I will go. I will always cherish the mem'ries of our visits. They linger like a beautiful dream.'

She never returned to reclaim her writing and a little while later, I found that her friend had been killed in Vietnam. Somehow I feel that they have found each other. Her writing has been a great source of inspiration for me, as well as my students."

Morgan and Clay stood transfixed, their arms entwined and their eyes riveted on Leonard, who had pushed himself out of his chair and, with a pair of tongs, had placed a large split log on the fire.

Turning ever so slowly and with his face caught in the brightening fire he said softly, "Morgan, you and Clay share a single soul."

The silence that followed was suddenly broken by the tinkling of a bell announcing that Claire's table was being set for breakfast.

"Before we go," Morgan said, exchanging glances with Clay, "as we were returning to the house last night, we heard this low moaning wail coming from the direction of the stones. All of us heard it and it frightened me badly. It was a quiet evening with no wind."

"Yes, and it wasn't an animal, at least any animal that I've ever heard," Clay enjoined.

Leonard studied them both carefully. "The stones, like other objects we encounter in nature, are monuments to spirit," he said at last. "They are living things, living entities if you will. No, not living in the way that we are accustomed to using the word. But living in the sense that they are storehouses of psychic energy that embody myriad possibilities seeking some form of individual expression."

While Leonard talked, Clay had placed another log and several pieces of kindling on the fire. For a moment, the room brightened as the flames quickly consumed the dry tinder. He returned, carrying a picture that had captured his attention.

"I don't believe we've talked about your one soul belief before," Morgan said somewhat hesitantly.

"No I haven't, but we must not keep Claire waiting. Her breakfasts are her passion."

"Is this you in this picture?" Clay asked, holding a framed photograph and handing it to Leonard, who was in the process of raising himself from his chair.

"Yes, may I see?" Morgan asked, eagerly stretching out her hand. "Leonard, that can't be you. This looks like a daguerreotype. It must have been taken over a century ago." Reaching for her glasses on top the piano, Morgan studied the photograph intently. "And who is this woman standing beside you, Clay?" Morgan's voice trembled as she spoke, "she looks... she looks like the woman in the patio door at our cottage in Stratford." Reaching for Clay's hand, she searched Leonard's face for an answer.

"Yes, it's me," Leonard said after a long pause. "And the woman is Claire."

The bleating of sheep in a far off pasture was the only sound to disturb the quiet of the morning. The tree-shaded Stour that flowed silently at the back of Primrose House looked glass-like as Morgan and Clay wandered along the river path under the pale morning sun. The faint smell of wood smoke hung on the moist air and a sudden soft breeze showered them with a flurry of yellow, gold and red leaves.

"The grass is wet," Clay said absently, picking up a leaf and twirling the stem in his fingers. Morgan, who had been quietly walking with her arm through his, looked up and nodded.

Her mind, however, was elsewhere. The note that Leonard had read had touched her deeply. It had captured a feeling that she had expressed to herself many times. And the photograph of Leonard and Claire. My God! Her head throbbed and she gently rubbed her forehead. *Are we deceiving ourselves?* she cried out to herself. *Are Clay and I living some bizarre illusion?*

Struggling to regain her composure, Morgan squeezed Clay's arm to her side.

"Do you think the people we've met, the places we've visited, the conversations we've had, are all a dream?" Morgan asked, giving Clay an imploring look. "Clay, are we dreaming? Will we wake up and find ourselves back in St. Paul?"

Clay, sensing Morgan's discomfort, stopped and cupped her face in his hands.

"No, honey," he said, trying hard to sound convincing. "But I know my understanding of what appears to be real and what appears to be illusion has undergone a profound change. But I don't know if what I've come to believe could stand intense cross examination."

"What is it that we believe?" Morgan asked, laying her head on Clay's shoulder.

They stood under an ancient oak tree, its rust-colored leaves heavy with acorns. Two white swans, who had been gliding silently alongside them, also stopped and began circling in the unruffled surface of the water.

"My mother," Clay said after a long pause "who taught Sunday School for many years, was fond of telling us that our thoughts create the mansion in which we will eventually spend our eternity." Morgan tightened her hold on Clay's arm. "It would seem," Clay continued, his eyes following the circling swans, "that our sense or reality has been seriously questioned. Our heaven, nirvana, Shangri-la or whatever we choose to call it, seems not to exist in some far off corner of the galaxy; it exists just beyond the reach of our senses, but not beyond the reach of our minds. Hillary's experience with the rose was not a dream, but a reality. And we're not dreaming either."

The clanging of the ship's bell hanging on a post near the rear door of Primrose House broke the attending silence and announced that lunch was about to be served. Chilled and hurrying back along the leaf-blanketed path, Morgan and Clay entered the warm, oak-paneled kitchen that was filled with the aroma of freshly-baked bread.

"I love that fragrance," Morgan said, rubbing her hands and warming herself before the fire that was cheerily burning in a large open fireplace.

"Our mornings are chill and if you don't dress warm you'll catch your death," Claire admonished, her face showing a broad smile. "And I must apologize for the interruption this morning before Leonard and Theo left for Oxford," Claire continued, gently setting three blue and white earthenware plates on the circular oak pedestal table. "I know that Leonard's response to the photograph deserved a far greater explanation than what we were able to give between my dear friend and neighbor Bess McGregor's visit and Leonard's and Theo's departure. Bess would not be dissuaded. She has a brother living in the states, a town in Iowa, Atlantic I believe, and when she rang me up this morning and asked if you had arrived, nothing except a serious accident would have kept her from calling this morning. But we can continue our talk about the photograph after lunch. Now, would you like coffee or tea?"

A piercing east wind whistled down the chimney and rattled the rain-streaked windows of the music room. "What would you like to hear, honey?" Morgan asked, seating herself on the piano bench. She turned so that she faced Clay, who had taken up residence in an overstuffed chair near the fire and was studying the photograph he had discovered earlier.

"I hadn't noticed it before," Clay said, giving Morgan a surprised look, "but this picture of Leonard and Claire seems to have been taken in front of the cottage we stayed in in Stratford."

"Yes," Morgan agreed in a voice just above a whisper. Turning, she placed her fingers on the keys.

The melodious sound of *Sentimental Journey* tempered the sound of the rain pelting the windows. Except for the mellow light of a table lamp alongside Clay and the flickering firelight, the room had grown dark.

"What is it about that cottage?" Clay remarked absently, leaning back in his chair and rubbing his eyes.

"We will know in a moment," Morgan said as she finished playing. "I hear her coming down the hall."

"You play beautifully, Morgan," Claire said, appearing in the doorway carrying a steaming pot of tea and three cups. "I remember it was a popular song during the war, 1944 or 1945, I believe."

"It's one of our favorites," Morgan said, getting up and taking an overstuffed chair next to Clay.

"Yes, we lost so many in that war," Claire's eyes clouded a bit as she pulled a wing-backed chair around to face her guests.

"Well, on a more cheery note, how do you and Clay find Oxford, a bit of a challenge I imagine?"

"We love it," Morgan said, leaning forward, her arms resting on her knees. "The pale stone buildings with their colorful roofs make for wonderfully scenic postcards. And the Bodleian Library, it simply defies description. There must be several million volumes available for study. And we were told during our tour that the zeal for knowledge among the early students was so voracious that books had to be chained to the shelves in the library."

"Yes," Clay interjected, "and at nine every evening we hear the sound of bells tolling 101 times. Do you know why?"

"Yes," Claire said, "they toll in rememberance of the 101 students who were the first to be enrolled in Oxford and, although Oxford is a city of trashy bulletin boards, there *is* a touch of the eternal about it."

"I had no idea there were so many colleges and so few students at Oxford, few at least by American standards," Morgan said with a bit of a sigh. "I think I heard a figure of ten thousand. Most American universities harbor well over fifty thousand students."

"We have compulsory tea at three," Claire said, smiling as she poured steaming tea through a strainer into three waiting cups. "Yes, Morgan, we are a bit old fashioned by American standards, but there are those, Theo and Leonard included, who see our schools as nurseries, taking substantially blank minds and instilling in them the love of learning. Such an ideal would be a bit illusive, I would think, when thousands of curious minds are sandwiched in one institution. But I suspect that both of you are impatient to learn about the photograph that Clay discovered on the table in back of the sofa," Claire continued, gingerly taking a sip of tea. "Well, let me begin by telling you that the cottage you stayed in in Stratford was my girlhood home. I can't tell you how many wonderful memories I have of growing up there. My father was a solicitor and my mother kept house. At night when my father was away, she would sit with us by the fire and lamp and enthrall us with stories of fairies, lost worlds, and mysterious disappearances."

"Us?" Morgan interrupted, giving Claire a bemused look.

"I had a brother whom I loved very much. He died of consumption, a horrid disease, soon after his eleventh birthday."

Claire had a habit of tilting her head and looking upward when responding to a question and she did so now.

"My mother," she continued slowly, "was what one would call a gnostic. She believed that we live in a prison planet filled with misfortunes and incurable problems. When friends visited, the conversation would invariably lead to how our souls, which contained the spark of the creator, had become entrapped in a pool of irrational matter. In the evenings, seated by the fire, she would enflame our imaginations with stories of wonders that she said existed just beyond the reach of our physical senses. Our home is not on this plane, she would say, but our underdeveloped and somewhat primitive senses bind us to a reality that is illusionary. Beyond our notions of time and space exist worlds where there is beauty, harmony, and balance, where souls find their essence, peace, contentment and fulfillment."

Except for the ticking of a Napoleon-style clock resting comfortably on the fireplace mantle and the occasional snap of a log burning cheerily in the fireplace, the room grew silent.

"Your mother must have been an exceptional person," Clay said softly.

"She was indeed," Claire answered. "My father's beliefs, if he had any, were never shared with us, but he never interfered with or showed disrespect for mother's beliefs."

"Did your mother say how one enters these heaven-like realms?" Morgan asked, wrapping a forest green afghan around her as if she had felt a sudden chill.

"Yes," Claire replied, her voice taking on a measured tone. "She said that for us to visit at will these wonderfully peaceful worlds, we must first believe that these worlds do indeed exist and that our minds are capable of entering them. However, she was always quick to point out that we simply do not languish or loiter in our new-found existence in a state of protracted bliss. No, we make ourselves useful. We bring some skill or gift to the table that the community needs or finds useful. So above, so below, so to speak."

"But exactly how does one enter these realms?" Morgan persisted, giving Clay a quick questioning look.

"The key, as I said, is to believe that they exist. I'm sure that you and Clay have desired something or you wanted something to happen so badly that it consumed all of your waking thoughts. And possibly a day, a week, or even a year later, what you desired happened. As a people, we have not yet fully recognized what a powerful energy force a single thought is. It is the force of thought that can satisfy a need or desire or create a beacon that can guide us to where we want to be. Everything we see around us began with a single thought. But to answer your question more fully, Morgan, to experience the wonders of thought creation, we must be willing to probe deep within our inner selves. Not everyone is willing to do so, but when we do, we awaken the universal mind that exists in each one of us. It is through the discovery and contact with this creative consciousness that wondrous worlds and realms emerge. However, as I know you both know, not everyone is equipped to embark on such quests—either because they lack the desire to know themselves or because they do not yet possess the perceptive and intuitive powers necessary for seriously exploring one's inner being."

"Yes," Morgan said, her eyes narrowing thoughtfully, "we often are blind to our true interests, aren't we? We seem to live lives precariously supported by style rather than the content of our being."

"Precisely," Claire said, giving Morgan a sharp look, "but I have strayed a bit from the cottage at Stratford. The cottage, I'm happy to tell you, at one time was owned by your ancestor, John Barnett."

Morgan caught her breath. *What else does this woman know*, Morgan asked herself. *I can't believe that what she is sharing is simply a bundle of miscellaneous recollections. There is a method and a purpose to everything Clay and I have experienced. I knew it!* She felt herself shivering inside. Gently rubbing her forehead, she became aware that the room had grown quiet and that both Clay and Claire were looking at her.

"I'm sorry," she said, returning Claire's studied look. "Please continue."

"Are you alright, honey?" Clay asked, getting up. Standing behind Morgan, he began to massage her shoulders.

"I'm fine, really I am," she said, looking up into Clay's face and smiling. "Claire's comment that John Barnett owned the cottage we stayed in caught me by surprise that's all."

"Yes," Claire continued, your ancestor, John, was also a gnostic and a possessor, like my mother, of secret knowledge. He, along with his friends who were adherants to hermetic doctrines, believed that the blue stones that we visited possessed magical powers and that they were one of many of nature's doorways or entrances into parallel worlds."

The sudden appearance of a black and white angora cat that leapt into Claire's lap startled both Morgan and Clay.

"I'm sorry," Claire said, her voice betraying a bit of amusement, "this is Penelope. She is the most eccentric thing. She may be gone for several days and then all of a sudden she appears out of nowhere."

"May I hold her?" Morgan asked, holding out her hands and giving Clay a knowing look over the rims of her glasses.

"Yes," Clay said teasingly, "cats are to Morgan what lap dogs are to jeweled women."

"Well, Penelope is a dear," Claire said, giving her cat a loving look. "But you may want to keep the afghan on your lap; she does shed a bit, and I would imagine your tea is ice cold. If you will excuse me I'll make a fresh pot and bring a saucer of milk for our newly arrived guest."

"It's still raining," Clay said, somewhat absently as he placed another log on the fire. "I wonder if Leonard and Theo have made it back to Oxford."

"Probably," Morgan quietly said, slowly stroking Penelope's soft, silk-like fur.

"Honey," Clay began, walking back to his chair, "what..." He didn't finish. Claire stood in the doorway, carrying a tray containing a steaming pot of tea, several tasty-looking scones, and a saucer of milk.

"I thought you both could use a bit of nourishment on this melancholy afternoon," she said brightly. "It's one of our harmless customs."

"And a much appreciated one, I may add," Clay said, taking the tray from her.

"I baked a pan this morning," Claire said, placing the saucer of milk down beside her chair. "I thought Abigail and Paddy would be dropping by this afternoon, but she called to say that Paddy was down with a chest cold and that he would require some looking after."

"These scones are delicious," Morgan said between bites. "Do I taste a bit of cardumum?"

"You do indeed."

"My mother used to make bread with cardumum in it," Clay said approvingly. "I had given up ever tasting anything like it again."

"Well, you've come a long way and we shan't disappoint you, but to return to our discussion."

"Yes, about the photograph," Morgan said, setting her cup and saucer down on the chairside table. "Leonard would admit only that it was you in the picture, but nothing more. I imagine he wanted you to provide the explanation."

"Yes," Claire replied, smiling as if she had recalled some happy event. "Well, simply put, when a person is able to travel between worlds, that is if the mind is unchained and free to soar and experience the beauties and wonders that exist beyond the scope of our senses, we are also free to appear as young or as old as we wish."

"But why bother coming back when you have found your Elysium?" Clay asked, leaning forward, his hands folded in front of him.

"Yes, why on earth would anyone want to return?" Morgan asked, giving Clay a look of disbelief.

There was a pause as Claire poured hot tea into their empty cups. "We choose to return" she said, looking up and smiling after setting the pot down on the tray, "to help others realize that they, too, can experience other worlds and that these worlds await their coming. Leonard and Theo have guided you, of course, but there have been others. Mrs. Michem, who you know as the cleaning lady at Centre, is the wife of Duncan Alister, the founder of your Centre College. And, of course, Archibald and the Beechams."

"And who are you?" Morgan asked softly, her eyes filling with tears.

"I'm simply a person who had the good fortune of being born to a mother who encouraged me not to unconditionally rely on my senses. To ascribe infallability to our senses is folly, she would say. Doubting the imposed conventions of society is always the starting point toward wisdom."

"It was you in the patio door of the cottage, wasn't it?" Clay asked, giving Claire a weak smile.

Claire nodded. "But on a lighter note," she said, getting up and taking their cups and setting them down on the tray. I have gifts for both of you, and Clay, if you would be so kind as to turn on the floor lamp beside you, I will retrieve them from my apartment."

Morgan and Clay exchanged questioning glances. "Honey, it's a gift just being here," Clay said, rising from his chair. "I don't think we should accept..." He didn't finish.

Claire, who had been gone but a moment, returned carrying the black lacquered box and a small package wrapped in crimson paper. Morgan sat silent as Claire placed the box in her hands.

"And this package is for you, Clay, and I would ask that you open yours first."

The satin-like paper peeled back to disclose a small, ivory case in which rested a pale gray pearl ring cast in a bluish overtone. When turned so that the light struck it at an angle, the pearl revealed the presence of a scarab. Clay sat silent as he and Morgan examined the ring with a mixture of surprise and studied fascination.

"It's beautiful, Claire," he said, looking up. "I'm sorry I have no words to describe my feeling and appreciation except, why?"

Claire nodded, but didn't answer.

"Is it a gift when the receiver already knows the content?" she asked. Her eyes shone with amusement as she met Morgan's steady gaze.

"Is it the scarab necklace that we discovered in the cottage?" Morgan asked, somewhat hesitantly as she lifted the cover.

"Yes."

Gently removing the crystal scarab and its gold chain from its black velvet cushion, Morgan studied it for several long moments. The rain had stopped and except for the ticking of the clock, the room was eerily silent.

"I don't undersand," she said at last, giving Claire an appreciative, but questioning look.

"The scarab necklace belonged to John Barnett," Claire said, taking a deep breath. "Like others who belonged to gnostic orders, he believed that a loving God would not place his charges in a prison such as exists on earth. In your Speculative Religion classes, Morgan, I'm sure you touched on gnostic beliefs and teachings. But in brief, the root of gnostic belief is that love, unity, and harmony exist in worlds that parallel the one we currently occupy. These worlds are God's true creations and we enter and experience their beauty and wonder through our revelationary thoughts, dreams, and visions."

"Do you mean permanently enter?" Clay asked, giving Claire a furrowed look.

"Yes."

There was an awkward pause as Morgan left her chair and stood near the window looking out into the darkness. Gnosticism is what I came to Oxford to learn more about, she said to herself as she watched a drop of water slowly make its way down the windowpane. *Are we like this drop of water? she wondered. Are we destined to follow a path of least resistance and end up being absorbed into the ground?*

"Isn't it interesting," she asked, turning and returning to her chair, "that the word 'liberation' has come to mean freeing oneself from the restrictions of our material environment. Rarely do we hear the word applied to the mind."

"Yes, please go on," Claire said, pouring hot tea into their cups.

"In my classes," Morgan continued, taking her cup from Claire's outstretched hand, "we discuss the mysterious disappearances of thousands of people each year. Disappearances that involve foul play aside, there are many instances where people have unaccountably vanished within sight of others. Where do they go?"

"And what do you tell them?" Claire asked gently, cradling her cup in both hands while she slowly sipped her tea.

"I don't tell them, they tell me," Morgan said, her voice taking on a wistful tone. "I simply ask them to use their imaginations to create a world that would meet all their needs, desires, and values. Interestingly, some would create a world similar to what you have already described Claire, while others are perfectly comfortable in simply recreating a world we are used to seeing, with more of its earthy pleasures, of course. I suggest to them that a mind, free to imagine, to soar above the conventions of our world, may one day find itself in the very place it has so imagined and dreamed about."

Morgan stopped to set down the cup of tea she was holding. "I'm sorry," she said, "I've been rambling. Claire, you were saying that this scarab necklace belonged to John Barnett."

"Yes, well as you probably know, to the ancient Egyptians the scarab symbolized the invisible creative force that authored everything seen and unseen. It was worn as a means of assuring both protection and immortality. When John Barnett left for America, he left the scarab with my mother's ancestors. Eventually it was passed down to her and to me. We knew you would come for it some day."

The room again grew quiet. Morgan noticed that the fire that had burned so brightly earlier had reduced to a scattering of glowing coals. The room seemed colder.

"There's a card attached to the underside of the cover," Morgan said, shifting her gaze from the coals to the box that rested on her lap. Gently removing it, she handed it to Claire. "I'm afraid my French is more than a little rusty. Can you translate it for us?"

"*Ill est temps de rentrer*. It means it's time to go home."

Chapter 11

The Homecoming

A grey, chilling mist had settled over the moor-like countryside, obscuring all but the tops of the wave-like hills. From time to time, a farmhouse or a stone church would suddenly appear, wraithlike, beside the road and disappear just as quickly.

"I hope the agonizing slowness of my driving doesn't bother you," Claire said, giving Morgan a demur look while holding the steering wheel in a vise-like grip.

"No, but I've noticed that you have a strip of red flannel stuck to the speedometer at thirty-five miles per hour," Clay said dryly, looking up from the map he was studying in the back seat.

"Yes, it helps me regulate my speed. Abigail and Paddy dislike accompanying me in the car even at this pace."

"And why is that?" Morgan asked.

"Well," Claire began and then paused. "You see I have a tendency to run over things, not that I try to, mind, but I feel almost certain that we will meet some domestic or wild animal during the course of our trip. Unfortunately, animals seem to have a partiality for the roads that I travel."

"Have you struck an animal lately?" Morgan asked, giving Claire a frowning smile.

"Last week I ran over Mr. Tedder's goat. He had chewed his tether in two and was belligerently standing in the middle of the road daring me to strike him. I dealt him a staggering blow. It was a dreadful experience."

"About our destination," Clay said, giving Morgan an amused look. I can't find Little Coxwell on the map."

"Yes, well you remember we talked about how thoughts can author creations well beyond what we normally see, hear and feel and how our recurring dreams are connected to our longings and innermost desires?"

"Yes," Morgan said, "But how do our thoughts and dreams relate to a place like Little Coxwell?"

"You won't find Little Coxwell on the map, Clay," Claire said, turning her head slightly in Clay's direction. Morgan, who had turned in her seat to face Claire, gave Clay a brief, but questioning look.

"Little Coxwell exists, but not in the way one might think. I suspect as male and female splinters of the same soul you have experienced similar dreams and visions and your thoughts have frequently centered on a place where love, peace, and beauty abound," Claire said, nodding as if to emphasize her point.

With her eyes fixed uneasily on the road ahead, she continued. "Morgan, you mentioned last night that you felt that imagination was a gift from God. And a fabulous gift it is. As you two have discovered, it awakens and excites the senses into thinking that very little in this world is truly impossible. Morgan, I would assume that when you were laboring at your studies you never really thought you would someday hold a professorship at a prestigious college. And Clay, I'm sure the same can be said for you. What you both imagined did indeed come true. Now, as to Little Coxwell. You're here at this moment because your wonderfully fertile imaginations have allowed you both to free yourselves from the ordinary and day-to-day realities that tend to suffocate our being. Because you share a single soul, each of you over the years has, sometimes knowingly, often unknowingly, projected a scene or a desired reality on the mind screen of the other. The desires are so real and the combined thoughts so incredibly powerful that the shared image becomes real."

"I understand how two people can embrace the same feelings and desires," Clay said, somewhat cautiously, "but sharing a single soul?"

"Yes, accepting the view that we share our sanctum with another person does not come without a struggle with long held beliefs and traditions," Claire said, turning and giving Clay a controlled smile.

"Do you mean that *every* person living shares their soul with someone else?" Morgan asked, giving Claire a studied look.

"Everyone who enters a realm, whether it be the one we currently occupy or some other, shares a soul with someone else."

Morgan sensed an unmistakable feeling of urgency in Claire's words. Casually spoken, they nevertheless carried an implicit, impelling meaning. From the look on Clay's face, she knew Clay had sensed it too. Then she remembered something her grandfather had said to her on the eve of her graduation from college. 'As a teacher you will always find reasoning under assault. It's one of life's annoyances. But truth needs no justification.' Was this truth, she wondered, or an absurdity passed off as truth? Aware that Clay had touched her shoulder she turned sideways to face Claire, who was smiling knowingly.

"Yes," Claire said softly, "we've all shared those same feelings. It's not absurd to believe that the world rests on the foundation of polar opposites, light and dark, right and left, rest and motion, order and chaos and of course, male and female. Although there is a few years difference in your ages, you and Clay agreed to revisit this realm so that each of you could work with a specific set of predetermined problems, problems when solved would contribute to your soul's overall evolution and progression."

"Are you saying that between lives we are *forced* to take an unvarnished inventory of ourselves?" Morgan asked thoughtfully, her forefinger resting under her chin.

"Not forced," Claire returned. "Nothing in the universe is stronger than your individual will. You control your will, no one else. Some souls choose to take stock of themselves and make the necessary adjustments for their soul's evolution. Others may not. Unfortunately we see and feel the actions of those who do not every day of our lives."

"Am I right in assuming that Morgan and I have, from the very beginning, shared a single soul?" Clay asked, leaning forward with his folded arms resting across the top of Morgan's seat.

"Yes," Claire answered, emitting a half laugh. "Before re-entering this realm, you agreed to eventually find each other, which of course, you did. Each of us is equipped with a mysterious homing sense which allows us to discover our other self, if indeed he or she has opted to join the other, which is not always the case. Sometimes one or the other may decide to experience the wonders of other realms, but each is forever joined by an unbreakable silver cord. Together, you and Clay have decided that your soul's progression would be best served by creating a realm where unity and harmony, peace and beauty exist in unbounded measure. Each shared soul, I should add, has the capacity for creating its own realms according to its needs and desires, but few do because of the ever-present reluctance to allow the mind to explore itself. Of course nothing of value is gained easily, and anyone who embarks on a voyage of discovery, especially the kind that may prove unsettling to established beliefs and conventions, may loose long held and cherished friendships. Life, however, should not be allowed to rust away."

"I confess that the notion of a shared soul is a compelling thought," Morgan said, shifting her gaze from the road to Claire. "Interesting, too, is how the term 'soul mate', if that's what you mean by shared soul, has crept into the vernacular. I wonder if people really know what they mean when they refer to themselves as being a 'soul mate' to someone?"

"In most instances, I think not," Claire replied, giving Morgan a raised eyebrow look. "I fancy the term has as many interpretations as there are people-few of which are terribly illuminating."

"Sharing one's soul with someone implies a timeless, unaltered state, doesn't it?" Morgan said in a voice just above a whisper.

"Yes, I'm afraid one hears the term soul mate used to blanket everything from an outwardly-convincing attraction to a mild infatuation. It may be that two people love each other and think they belong together, but it doesn't necessarily mean that they share the same soul. It is the depth of their constant and combined love that gives meaning to the term shared soul. However, one should not become discouraged if in any given lifetime he or she is unable to discover their, let's say, 'soul mate.' There are times when two people will decide to go their separate ways either in the same or a separate lifetime. The tether remains intact regardless. Even without the other, a shared soul is never truly alone."

The grey mist continued to envelop the undulating landscape and spots of rain began to appear on the windshield. They had driven several miles in silence, each preoccupied with their own thoughts.

"I'm sorry," Claire said at last, flipping the switch that activated the windshield wipers. "I have a tendency to ramble. What I've shared with you were thoughts that my mother and others have shared and as we know, ideas and thoughts that make a strong impression on us when we are young are rarely erased by education or maturity."

"What you've said seems enduringly simple," Morgan said, leaning her head against the window and fixing Claire with a thoughtful gaze.

"Yes," Claire replied softly, nodding her head. It's not surprising, given the elevated state of your soul, that you have created Little Coxwell as have others you will meet there. Your dreams have taken you there. Now it's time to experience, while you're fully awake, what you have created in your dreams."

"I don't understand, Claire. Are you telling us that Little Coxwell exists as an actual place or are you saying it exists, but we see it as if we were watching a movie?" Morgan asked in a voice rising with excitement.

"Little Coxwell exists and its presence is just as real and solid as anything that we have experienced in this or any other lifetime. But we're coming to the end of our journey. Watch for a gate which will appear just beyond that grove of trees to the left."

An avenue of stately oaks, their branches knarled and twisted, formed a leafy, rusty-brown canopy over the lane-like road that lay ahead. Slowly disappearing in the mist behind them were two, tall ancient-looking stone pillars and plain, double barred wrought iron gate which had been opened at their approach by a man standing at the entrance. The collar of his yellow rain slicker was turned up so that it partially obscured his face. Slowing, Claire smiled and waved to the man, who Morgan noticed while looking back toward the gate, had disappeared.

"Clay, did you think the man who opened the gate looked familiar?" Morgan asked in a deliberate tone as she turned in her seat to face him.

"Vaguely. At first I thought he was the person we saw at Archibald's book store, but that person was blind so it couldn't have been."

"It was the same man. It was his eyes. I'm sure of it. But the man at the gate wasn't blind." Morgan turned, her eyes fixed on the road ahead. "It was the same man we saw in the bookstore, wasn't it, Claire?"

"Yes."

Clay, who had been noisily attempting to refold two uncooperative road maps, heard Morgan catch her breath. Out of the mist loomed a tall, grey standing stone, its surface clothed in tufts of green moss. Alongside the pockmarked stone, the lane-like road had come to an abrupt end.

"We will need to go the rest of the way on foot," Claire said, braking to a crunching stop on the hard gravel. "Take the luggage that you can carry comfortably. The remainder, we will retrieve later. That tree-shaded footpath to our right will take us to Little Coxwell."

"I can't believe this," Morgan said, nervously buttoning her short, black leather coat. "I can't believe we're here and I'm not sure I can trust what I'm feeling."

"Neither can I," Clay agreed, catching his breath and reaching in the back seat for his jacket. "Can we go back if we decide to?"

"Certainly, any time you and Morgan wish to leave you may do so. There are few who come this far who aren't beset with a host of anxieties and fears. We would not expect otherwise."

They stood motionless for a long moment, their eyes fixed on the wandering foot path that would quickly disappear in the chill, misty quietness of the open woods.

"Should we go back?" Clay asked uneasily, tightening his hold around Morgan's waist. At that moment, the muffled pealing of a bell broke the silence.

"It's our schoolbell at Little Coxwell," Claire said, reassuringly. "It summons the children back to their studies."

For a long moment, Morgan and Clay searched each other's faces. Then, as if some unseen communication had passed between them, they nodded and turned toward Claire who, smiling, took each of their hands in hers.

The fine mist that had obscured all but the spindly birch trees and thorny hawthorns that accompanied them for much of their walk, had mysteriously dissolved as they reached the crest of an arched stone bridge, its ancient stones covered by patches of grey and black lichen. Stopping on the bridge, they noticed that a soft wind had scattered the last of the translucent vapors. Before them, standing under a bright sun, was a picturesque village nestled in the folds of a lush valley bordered by gently sloping emerald colored hills. For what seemed an eternity, Morgan and Clay stood motionless, enthralled by the tranquil beauty of the scene that lay before them. Long moments of silence passed before any of them spoke.

"Welcome to Little Coxwell," Claire said, at last starting them along the broad, sloping tree-canopied lane that led to a paved, arching street, flanked by neat, whitewashed and honey colored stone cottages, their walls festooned with clinging vines and and colorful climbing flowers. People working in the yards of their thatched and russet-colored slate-roofed homes doffed their caps or waved as they passed.

Morgan stopped and closed her eyes tightly. Taking a deep breath, she felt herself stiffen. Her head throbbed and the tingling sensation in her fingers had returned. *This can't be happening to us*, she said to herself. *I feel...I feel as if I'm losing myself...I'm not myself...I'm being aborbed...into what!*

Long forgotten memories flashed through her mind. Suddenly, she was back at her grandparent's house. The clasp on the old, upstairs trunk was broken and in it among her mother's souvenirs she had found an old lace valentine that still carried the haunting fragrance of lilac. At the bottom, she remembered, were the words that her father had penned. 'It matters not that seasons pass. We two are one. Our journey here is near its end and the best is yet to come'.

Bursting into tears, she felt Clay's arms encircling her. "Honey," he began. "Let's go back, I..." He didn't finish.

Regaining control, Morgan pulled back and and placed her finger across his lips. "No, my dear," she said, smiling through her tears. "I'm fine now. I understand." Looking up into Clay's eyes, she became aware that her headache was gone, as was the tingling sensation in her fingers.

"I'm sorry, Claire," Morgan said, turning and reaching for her hand. "It all seems like a dream. Part of me accepts what I'm seeing and feeling and part of me senses that we will wake up and find ourselves back in our cottage in Oxford."

Clay, who had been studying Morgan intently, breathed a heavy sigh. Taking out his handerchief, he gently wiped Morgan's cheek.

"I think I understand too," he said softly, giving Morgan a knowing look. "You were somewhere else, weren't you?"

"Yes."

"You found a letter in your parents' trunk," Clay said, in a low voice.

"Yes, a valentine."

Clay nooded. There was a twinkle in his eyes.

Both Morgan and Clay noticed that Claire had strayed from their side and was standing several yards away, her eyes fixed on the overhanging branches of a large maple tree.

"The colors of autumn are beautiful, aren't they?" Morgan asked, taking Clay's hand and joining Claire, who had started to move up the street. The colors are so vivid, much more so than anything I've ever seen. When I've dreamed of such a place it's always been in the summer, but then, too, the colors have always been brilliant and alive."

"Our summers are not perpetual here," Claire said, giving Morgan a kindly smile. "We experience all the seasons that are common in other dimensions."

"Even snow?" Morgan asked, somewhat hesitantly.

"Even snow," Claire laughed.

Their stroll through the village took them past a large, open green upon which a cricket match was in progress. Beyond the green, the sun-dappled waters of a rippling river flowed lazily along its tree-lined, meandering course.

As they strolled along, Morgan marveled at the richness of what she was seeing and the peace and contentment she now felt. Harmony, yes. I feel a harmony with all things she said to herself, a smile creasing her lips. 'Self-originated' is how Claire had described it.

After they had walked for several minutes in silence, Morgan stopped and turned to Claire. "And why do I think I hear the chirping of birds?"

"Because you do. We have all manner of birds and animals that exist in other worlds—except rats and snakes. But you two must be hungry; it's nearly one o'clock and the village pub is just around the next corner."

"Is it the *Song O' The Winds?*" Clay asked, giving Morgan a hurried glance.

"Yes."

Ushered to a table near a hanging blackboard that announced the daily specials, both Morgan and Clay collapsed in their highbacked, wooden chairs. Claire, who had disappeared for a moment, reappeared carrying a steaming pot of tea and three earthen cups.

"There are numbers alongside the daily specials," Clay said, giving Claire a quizzical look.

"It's important that you understand their meaning," Claire said, patting Clay's hand and giving Morgan an amusing look. "They tell the customers how many of a certain food item can be ordered before the kitchen runs out."

Further conversation was interrupted by loud talk taking place at a nearby table.

"If Mrs. Bisset wants to idle away her hours crocheting

instead of tending to her garden, that I think is her business," a large man with a heavy shock of wiry black hair and
eyebrows to match was forcefully telling a white haired and
rather demure-looking woman who sat across from him.
"We must overlook the little unsettling behaviors of our
neighbors. Would you not agree, Mrs. Papers?"

It was evident that the woman sitting stiffly in her chair
was not to be dissuaded in her opinion. She continued to
meet his fixed stare with a look of serene indifference.

"That's Mr. Jameson Carstairs, known to everyone as
Jamy, and Penelope Papers," Claire said, her eyes shining
with amusement. "Whenever I return, I usually find them at
the same table discussing, not always tactfully, one of the
day's sufferances. He's the village florist. His shop on High
Street is filled with all sorts of colorful flowers and fra-
grances, and Penelope is the village's most accomplished
and deliberate gardener. Her roses, as well as her cabbages,
always take first prize in the fall's judging. As you can see,"
Claire added, touching Morgan's hand, "a high degree of
independent thought exists here and as a result feelings are
sometimes aroused and ventilated just as they are in our
more earthly dimension. Serious disagreements and irrita-
tions are handled by one of the village's barristers. But, as
you will see, we have no need of a constabulary here."

Earnest and determined conversation from nearby tables,
dissolving from time to time into bursts of laughter, drew
Morgan's attention as she surveyed the dining room.

"Who is that distinguished-looking man seated by the
bow window?" Morgan asked, turning toward Claire. "For
some strange reason I feel I know him."

"Yes," Clay said, his eyes drawn to the small, ruddy-faced
man with horn-rimmed glasses and a tweed, belted smoking
jacket and knickers. "He does seem familiar and then again
he doesn't. I don't know."

"The man is Owen Bates," Claire said, emptying a spoonful of sugar in her tea. "He is vicar of St. Andrew Church. Very well liked by all, I may add." As if anticipating Morgan's questionning look, Claire continued. "Yes, he is the same person that you and Clay found in the book at Stratford. He arrived here just about this time in 1939. But there are many others who have been here much longer. You see, things change here, but much more slowly than what we are accustomed to in our other existence."

"I don't understand," Clay said. "I don't understand how the people here in this room, not to say those living in the rest of the village, could agree to commit themselves to live together in some type of protracted harmony for what...decades, centuries? Over time, I would think there would come a revival of old desires and conventions. It's hard to think of a society that doesn't have at least one Judas goat."

Claire smiled. "Think about how many people we come in contact with that we really know. What do we really know about their hopes, dreams, desires, values? I daresay precious little, if anything at all. But, as you can see by looking around the room, there are those whose thoughts have connected in the ether and formed a reality that bonds them together for as long as they wish. Like attracts like. We can stay and continue to enjoy the peace and fulfillment that prevails or we can, by our desires and dreams, go on to other worlds which exist in a countless array of forms."

"More tea?" the waitress, attired in a plum-colored dress with a white apron, asked as she held a brown teapot over their empty cups.

"Yes, please," Morgan said, looking up and smiling. Claire and Clay shook their heads. "We can go back to whence we came or go forward to other realms. Is that what you mean?" Morgan asked, giving Claire a measured look.

"Yes, you and Clay can go back anytime you wish, but to return, as we have said, you must believe that Little Coxwell exists and that your experience here has been real. If doubt or disbelief overtakes, the gates to the village will disappear. Also, in order to return, one must be willing to subdue one's ego and all that it demands."

"And if we desire to go forward to higher realms?" Morgan persisted, taking a long sip of tea.

"There are no higher realms, only different realities, all of which exist in the mind," Claire replied, her face set in a kindly smile. "The mind authors our reality. To enter what the mind has created, we must, as we have said before, believe."

"Are you saying that we are, at this moment, living in our minds?" Morgan asked in a tone that was both deliberate and subdued.

"Yes."

For several long moments, neither Morgan, Clay nor Claire spoke. Finally Clay, leaning forward and folding his hands on the table, broke the silence.

"Tell us about the painting over the fireplace at Stratford," he said, "We thought the painting seemed old and it was crinkled in places, but the faces of the couple standing before the door of *Song O' The Winds* seemed freshly painted."

Claire returned Clay's steady look. "As I'm sure you have guessed, it was no accident that you and Morgan were encouraged to take lodging at the cottage at Stratford. You see, the cottage, do you recall its name? Yes, the Odyssey. Well, it has a unique and abiding purpose. There exists, within its ancient walls, a benign, but intelligent energy that delights in discovering the extent and quality of one's sixth sense, if you will. Some of the sounds you heard were no doubt discordant and disturbing, but they *were* heard, especially by you Morgan. But as we have said before, you and Clay share a single soul and while Clay was not always aware of the voices and sounds that you heard, he, nevertheless, has the capacity to do so as evidenced by the fact that we are here talking about the cottage and the painting over the fireplace. You see, persons who share a single soul are forever linked and wherever one goes, the other must follow."

"I think I need a glass of the strongest ale that the publican serves," Clay said, motioning to the waitress. Both Morgan and Claire shook their heads, but requested that their tea cups be refilled.

"But to continue," Claire said, slowly stirring a spoonful of sugar in her steaming cup. "The cottage that you occupied is but one of thousands of way stations that exist throughout the world. The fact that a person finds lodging in one of these, however, doesn't always mean that they will go on to eventually experience their nirvana or Shangri-la. Doubt or disbelief in the power of the mind often defeats their odyssey even before it begins."

"Who are the people in the painting?" Morgan asked, pursing her lips.

"Ronnie and Pamela Claiborne—a charming couple. He is the director of our village's playhouse and Pamela is principal of one of our three grammar schools. Ronnie is directing, and has a supporting role in Shakespeare's *Measure For Measure,* which I believe is scheduled to open next week."

"But we must be on our way," Claire said, suddenly getting to her feet. Sensing that Clay was was about to reach for his wallet, she sat back down, making a vague gesture. "I find myself doing the same thing on occasion, Clay. You see, we have no monetary system here, yet in the absence of both paper and coin as you will see, all our needs are met. But we must hurry. You, no doubt will want to spend the night and we will need to register you at the Waterford, a wonderfully cozy inn, facing the river with private baths. In addition, there are a number of people who want to meet you, including the irreproachable Miss Hillary Bowden."

"Ginger is an interesting name for a main street," Morgan said, as they proceeded along a somewhat narrow tree-lined avenue fronted on both sides by colorful stone and half-timbered, gabled shops.

"I imagine the name comes from the color of the cobblestones, don't you think?" Claire answered, stopping abruptly to wave at someone through a small paned window in which an irresistible variety of bake goods were enticingly displayed. "That's Ernest Journet. He has been supplying the village with wonderful treats ever since he fled France during the revolution. And that reminds me, records of all the residents, when they arrived, and the date of their departures are kept upstairs in the guildhall. The keeper of the records is Matthew Thornton, who we met at the gate."

The scarlet and gold leaves that carpeted the sidewalk and street shivered slightly at the urgings of a cool, but gentle wind.

"I have no words to describe my feelings," Morgan said, after they had walked a short distance in silence. "This street is so marvelously charming, there are so many varied and inviting shops and restaurants, and everyone is so friendly. I'm sorry, I wish I could express what I feel."

"There is no need to," Claire said, taking Morgan's arm. "But you and Clay have seen only a small part of the hustle-bustle that exists in Little Coxwell. There are all manners of clubs and organizations to excite one's interest. We have team sports such as we saw on the green, and on Sunday nights there is the customary band concert in the park that borders the duck pond just down the next street. And, oh yes, we also have a college for those whose passion runs to advanced study. I would imagine, Morgan, that a teaching position just might be available to you upon your request." Claire's finishing words were quietly spoken, so quietly that they sounded almost matter-of-fact.

Feeling that Claire had read her mind, Morgan blushed a bright pink. Secretly she had dreaded meeting Mrs. Simmons, thinking that she had, for some diabolical purpose, orchestrated the disquieting events they had experienced. Now she felt nothing but admiration for this wonderfully astute and unassuming woman who had lifted the veil and had given full flower to their consciousness. *For the first time in my life*, Morgan thought, *I'm experiencing, no, realizing, my true being.* She knew that Clay felt the same indescribable feeling of completeness. She remembered Leonard saying that 'entering a state of pure consciousness is our birthright. Pure happiness does not reside in the outside world, it lies within if we but search for it.' *Yes, and how can I describe the feeling of oneness and fulfillment that I feel*, she said to herself. Every moment is filled with beauty, contentment, and peace. As if awakening from a deep sleep, Morgan was faintly aware that Clay had put his arm around her shoulders drawing her close to him.

"Is there anything that Little Coxwell doesn't have?" Clay asked, looking down and giving Morgan an understanding look. Morgan had followed his eyes and she knew he had entered her thoughts.

"Well, we don't have need for hospsitals or doctors, although there are medical people residing here," Claire said, giving Clay a fleeting smile. "You see, everyone who comes to Little Coxwell brings some skill or artistry with them. Where a kind of previous training is not needed here, the college up on the hill offers an infinite number of courses to help the student discover other abilities. Everyone strives to be useful. We do, however, have people who are trained to assist and counsel others regarding new-found interests, as well as those who wish to move on to other realms. And then there are those, like me, who choose to assist, I like to use the word pilgrim, on their last and often the most anxious and defining leg of their journey that leads them to their Little Coxwells."

"I don't recall seeing a car," Clay said, slowly rubbing his chin. "Someone in the village must own a car."

"No, you will find no exhaust fumes in Little Coxwell. Locomotion is limited to walking, running, riding a bicycle, horseback riding, hitching a ride on a jaunting cart and, in the winter, a chair sled or a horsedrawn sleigh."

"What's a jaunting cart?" Clay asked, giving Claire a quizzical look.

"It's a simple, horse-drawn conveyance. The driver sits in front and the passengers sit on each side facing away from each other. In many ways, the pace of life is very slow here."

The afternoon light was beginning to dissolve into a blending of orange and purple hues as they turned off Ginger Street, with its beckoning shops, colorful signboards and flowerboxes, onto an arching street bordered by cozy, pale limestone and whitewashed houses and cottages whose windows glowed with a warm and inviting light.

"This is Ivy Street," Claire said. "As you can tell, many of the cottages along here are laced with vines. In some instances, our street names are not terribly original," she concluded with a wry smile.

Morgan, who had been walking with her arm through Clay's, suddenly turned, taking Clay with her. Peering at them from a dormered window resting under an eyebrow thatch of the cottage they had just passed, was the angelic face of a child.

"What expressive eyes," Morgan said as they continued their walk. "I don't know why I turned, but I'm glad I did. What a beautiful child. Strange, I have the feeling that... there was something familiar about her."

"I'm sure you two have met before," Claire said, giving Clay a knowing smile. "But Matthew Thornton lives along this street. If we hurry we might be able to catch him in his yard before the light fails and he's off to one of his organization meetings."

The snip, snip, snip sound of clippers came from alongside the bright yellow door that stood out in bold relief against the stark, white walls of a house roofed in russet slate. The light from two, large recessed and small-paned windows cast a warm glow on the flower beds and on the flower bordered path that led to the front entrance.

"Is that you, Matthew?" Claire called, her voice resounding on the crisp, still air.

"Yes, yes. Come ahead, I'm pruning my roses and it's a prickly job, especially in this failing light."

Both Morgan and Clay caught their breaths. The light from the window revealed the face of the sightless man that they had seen in Archibald's book store and had seen at the pillared gate only hours before. Morgan's hold on Clay's arm tightened.

"Matthew, I'd like you to meet the Ashtons, Morgan and Clay. This, my friends, is our irreplaceable keeper of the records, Matthew Thornton."

"I have to caution Claire from time to time about her reckless and totally unsupported assertions," Matthew said, standing and brushing off his knees while giving Claire an amusing smile. Removing his gloves, he clasped their hands in a firm handshake.

"I've not known Claire to exaggerate," Morgan said, giving Matthew a look of feigned innocence.

"And neither have I," Clay added firmly, giving Morgan's hand a squeeze. "But I believe we've met before. Not formally... at the bookstore in Petersfield. You had arrived just as we were leaving."

"Yes," Matthew responded in a voice distinctly British, "Archibald is an old friend and one of these days he will join us here in Little Coxwell. But for the moment, he is indispensible to hundreds of bibliophiles around the world. I trust you found his discourse on the blue stones a tempting thought, worthy of serious reflection?"

Matthew stood before them on the rusty, red brick path, his face half hidden in shadow. He was a tall, spare and somewhat stooped, square jawed man with thin lips and an aquiline nose. Under his tartan flat cap was a shock of pepper grey wiry hair that receded noticeably at the temples. There was, Morgan thought, a disarming charm about this man whose deep set eyes seemed to shine with amusement.

"Yes," Morgan replied, returning Matthew's steady look. "But ever since your arrival at the book store and your appearance at the gate, we have been struggling with how you have appeared to us in so many ways."

"You are referring to my sight or lack of it, of course?" Matthew replied, slowly stroking his chin. "Yes, well the explanation is astonishingly simple. You see, when one of our citizens leaves Little Coxwell on some errand or task, a condition or infirmity that they experienced while in their earthly realm returns. As you can see, the condition, whatever that may be, disappears upon our return."

In the deepening dusk, wisps of bluish white smoke drifted lazily from the chimneys of the cottages bordering the cobblestone street worn smooth by centuries of travel. Except for the voices of children playing in nearby yards and a nightbird's shrill cries, a hush had descended over Ivy Street. Undisturbed by passing zephyrs, the tantalizing smell of burning leaves hung heavily in the still air.

"But we must not loiter," Matthew said, giving Claire a hurried glance. "Before the light fails completely, we must show you a cottage that's located down this street just beyond the curve."

"Yes," Claire said, ushering them through the iron gate and out onto the road. "It belongs to friends of ours who have decided well...you will see for yourselves."

Morgan and Clay stood transfixed before a thatched, pale

stone cottage whose walls were enveloped in vines and climbing red and yellow roses. Two large, diamond-paned windows rested on each side of a heavy wooden door painted in tones of rusty red. Two upstairs diamond paned windows peeped out from under eyebrow thatch and wisps of nearly transparent smoke drifted from the two, tall brick chimneys that anchored each end of the roof. The windows glowed with a warm and cozy light.

Neither Clay nor Morgan spoke for several moments. Unaware that Matthew had left them, Morgan turned to find Claire standing well behind them, her hands thrust deeply into the pockets of her short coat.

"Would you like to see the interior?" Claire asked quietly as she walked up beside them.

"No," Morgan said softly, her head resting on Clay's shoulder. "We know what lies within. We have been here many times in our dreams."

"And who lives in the cottage now?" Clay asked.

"Duncan and Pauline Alister," Claire said, somewhat wistfully after a moment of silence.

It was then, for the first time, that they noticed a small unobtrusive sign in the yard. It read, *Available For Immediate Occupancy. Inquire Within.*

Epilogue

Little Coxwell continues to welcome other travelers. Leonard Crawford became a student in Advanced Philosophies at the college and Archibald Duncannon became the sole proprietor of the village's only rare bookstore.

Theopholis Weeks continues to irritate his students with his uncompromising attitude toward tardiness, but will eventually join his friends, becoming the village's head librarian.

Similarly, the Beechams, Howard and Ellie, too will also retire to Little Coxwell. Howard will accept an invitation to become the headmaster of the village's new grammer school and Ellie will spend her mornings teaching English at the college and her afternoons tending her flower garden.

Claire Simmons, however, will continue to occupy Primrose House, cheerfully welcoming those travellers who have begun their odyssey at the cottage at Stratford. Her duties require that she make frequent return visits to Little Coxwell.

The cottage at Stratford has remained unoccupied for eleven years. On a warm, rainy afternoon in May, the cottage welcomed its new guests, Christopher and Claudia Bancroft.

Except for numerous unaccountable sounds, which on several instances sounded like a woman's laughter, their stay was a pleasant one. Sitting before a low fire on their second evening, their attention was drawn to a painting that hung over the fireplace. It depicted an English village and its attending pub. The painting, they agreed, was old, but curiously, the faces of the dark haired man and the woman with blond hair standing outside the pub seemed freshly painted.

As had the Ashtons before them, they too had found a book bound in blue leather resting on the nearby desk. It bore no title, but a beautiful, cursive handwriting described the mysterious diappearances of forty-seven people, the first occurring in 1811. Paging through the book, the Bancrofts' attention had been drawn to the last entry. It described how, on their first visit to England eleven years before, an American couple from Minnesota had mysteriously disappeared while traveling by car between Oxford and Bath. At the very bottom of the last entry was a notation written by a different, but equally beautiful hand. It read simply, *The first step to better times is to imagine them.*